FREEDOM

To Harry and Adam

While this book is based on real characters and actual historical events,
some situations and people are fictional, created by the author.

Scholastic Children's Books,
Euston House, 24 Eversholt Street,
London NW1 1DB, UK

A division of Scholastic Ltd
London ~ New York ~ Toronto ~ Sydney ~ Auckland
Mexico City ~ New Delhi ~ Hong Kong

First published in the UK by Scholastic Ltd, 2018

ISBN 978 1407 18548 4

Printed and bound by CPI Group (UK) Ltd, Croydon, CR0 4YY

2 4 6 8 10 9 7 5 3 1

Papers used by Scholastic Children's Books
are made from wood grown in sustainable forests.

www.scholastic.co.uk

CATHERINE JOHNSON

FREEDOM

SCHOLASTIC

CHAPTER

1

JAMAICA, 1783
BARRATT HALL ESTATE

I swept the paths in the flower garden as if I was the devil cutting down every sinner in hell. But I kept my face cool as an evening breeze. No one would see my anger if I could help it. I screwed up my eyes to stop them prickling. I didn't want anyone to notice how hard I was trying not to think of Mamma and my baby sister Martha. Would they be on the wagon by now? I'd seen it arrive nearly an hour ago. Mamma had hugged me tight before I left for work, told me to be strong. I didn't want to let her go. I hugged Martha too but she was grizzling like she knew something was up and there was nothing in the world I could do for her.

I would probably never see them again.

Even so, I kept my eyes down, my anger bottled up. I didn't want Missis Palmer, the housekeeper, telling me my business, or worse one of the Barratts. Either the young master or the old mistress who liked to sit on the veranda with her parrot, Mr Bird, her hand resting on her long hardwood stick. Although the young master was callous, sharp-tongued and nasty, it was his mother, the old mistress who was worse. I gripped the broom tighter. On my right hand there were only four fingers. And while the old mistress hadn't chopped it off herself, she had stood by while Mr Bird took his great black beak, sharp as a machete, and pecked it clean off.

Last night the rain had come down heavy as

stones, now the hibiscus blooms carpeted the path in every shade of blue and purple, and my job was to sweep up every single one. The roses seemed to have enjoyed the drink and just opened up, white and pink; so much colour. I knew I should have felt joyful at the work of God's hand, but I did not.

Oh, I knew that working in the gardens was a nice, nice job. I knew I was lucky I didn't have to break my back in the fields with Mamma, cutting the sugar cane with baby Martha strapped to her back. So even though I wanted to walk through all the flower beds, stamping on everything, killing it all, I kept sweeping.

Old Thomas, the gardener, with his bent back and barely a hair on his head, called out to me. I looked up and he waved me over. I threw down the broom. He was taking a cutting from a lantana tree, holding the branch so tenderly it might have been a baby.

"This is the one, see, Nat? Cut the stem here where it fork." Old Thomas kissed his teeth. "Are you watching, Nathaniel? How you expect to learn?"

"Excuse me, sir," I said.

Thomas grinned, showing two teeth, one top, one bottom. He shook his head. "You think I don't know what you're thinking? Throwing a good broom like that when it don't do you no wrong!" He took a knife from his pocket with his free hand and cut the branch just so, like it was butter.

"You wan' end up like me?" He looked down at his right foot. Cut in two but healed up into half a foot long before I was born. Smooth brown skin patterned with darker scars. No toes.

"If the young massa or the overseer catch you before you find Maroon Town and freedom, then this what happen," he said. "You have a good job, decent job, 'member that. No whip on your young back if you careful."

"I know that, Mr Thomas, but—"

"No buts. You go wrong, you run away, they take off half your foot so you no run no more. You no listen to Massa, they whip you 'til the skin fall off your back. Maybe take off your ear, slit your nose so." He pointed his knife at me and I stepped back.

"Sorry, Mr Thomas."

"Don't be sorry. Listen. Learn. Your mother told me keep my eye fix 'pon you and so I do. You no worry about her or the pickney no more. You hear?

Them sold an' that the end of it." He tipped the straw hat back on his head and itched at his scalp. He looked serious. "An' you an' I know she probably better off far from here."

I didn't say anything. My eyes stung. I must have had some dust or something in the corner because I had to rub them with the back of my sleeve. I sniffed too. But I knew he was right. Since the old mistress had brought in a new overseer things had got worse for all of us. Earlier, when the wagon arrived, I heard the crying as folk said goodbye. I knew Mamma and my little sister would be gone before the sun rose any higher. Gone to work in a parish far from here on the south of the island.

Old Thomas shook his head. He snipped off an armful of yellow flowers from the lantana tree and piled them in my arms.

"Tek these to Missis Palmer. Go on with you, up to the house. Go the long way and you jus' might see the wagon pass at the long bend."

"Thank you, Mr Thomas!" I said, even though I had already started running.

But I was too late. The big six-wheeled cart carrying

Mamma, Martha and the others who'd been sold, was rolling down the palm-lined drive. It was almost at the gate. I dropped the flowers without thinking and waved and waved with both hands.

"Mamma!" I called out loud, and I swear I saw her head turn.

It came like a bolt of lightning. The blow across the back of my head sent me reeling. In an instant I was face down on the ground with a mouthful of dirt and a pain so hot and hard across the back of my scalp I thought my head had split right open.

"Pick those up. Horrid boy!"

It was the old mistress. She stood above me, a slight woman with a core of iron. She wore a dark cotton dress down to the ground and Mr Bird sat on her shoulder, a tiny chain around one scaly clawed foot. It regarded me with its yellow eye and opened its beak up wide and laughed its horrible laugh.

"Horrid boy! Horrid boy!" it screeched.

The mistress had dealt me a blow with her stick. Thomas had told me about the tree it was cut from. How they used to hang slaves in its branches before it fell down in a storm. How the gardener before him had cut a stick for the old master. And how that stick had done a deal of harm for a long time. To man and boy, woman and girl.

The old mistress swished away, with Mr Bird stretching its wings out.

"Horrible child," she said. "Waving your arms about like that."

"Horrid boy!" Mr Bird said again, and laughed some more. "Bones and blood! Bones and blood!"

My head felt like it was singing with pain. I got up without making a sound, even though I wanted to yell with the hurt of it. I stopped myself putting my hand up to the back of my head where I could feel the skin broken and something wet, blood maybe, trickling down the back of my neck.

I began picking up the flowers. I took my time, watching as the old mistress entered the big house and disappeared. I would not give her the pleasure of knowing how much she had hurt me. What did Mamma say? *Walk tall, they cannot hurt us. They have hurt us so hard and for so long. What more can one blow do?*

When I'd gathered them all up I walked towards the house, heading to the small kitchen door. From the open windows above I heard shouting. And not just shouting, neither. The young master was fairly raging at his mother. I wondered for a short moment why she did not use her stick on him.

"You had no right to decide which slaves we sell or which we keep!" the young master yelled. Then the sound of breaking glass. "I am in charge here, Mother. Not you!" Another crash. China smashing this time. Perhaps a vase? A chamber pot?

Missis Palmer the housekeeper saw me and snapped at me to come in. Her face was a mess of scowling. That woman could cut her eyes at you so sharp you could fall down dead. I thought to get away quick before she hit me too.

Just then there was another crash from upstairs. Missis Palmer clapped her hands and despatched Bets and Mary Two to clean up.

Bets shook her head. "I'm not going 'til that noise stop, not for nobody."

Missis Palmer spoke low, her voice dangerous.

"You better do as you're told, Betsy Barratt, or I'll see you're on the next wagon out of here to Mount Vernon along with the others!"

Betsy picked up the dustpan and left.

All I could think was Mount Vernon. That was where Mamma and Martha were going.

"Have you no brains, Nathaniel? Are your wits shotten? I don't want those here!" Missis Palmer bought her hand down so hard on the tabletop that the flowers jumped. The pain in my head throbbed harder.

"And stop your bleeding all over my kitchen floor. It only clean two minutes!"

CHAPTER

I was sitting on the low wall by the kitchen garden while Old Thomas cleaned up the cut on my head with some chaney-root water. He was singing while he cleaned, a sad song.

"Long time, I no see Li-za," he sang. I wished he would stop as it was making me sad too, thinking about Mamma.

"Why is it we are the slaves and they are our masters?" I asked. "Are they different from us? Underneath?"

Thomas laughed. "They the same. But they tell us – and themselves – a load of stories that we deserve nothing else. But really it's jus' because they hold the ships and the whips and the guns."

"So if we held them they'd be our slaves?"

Thomas frowned. "Ain't no merit in making any man a slave of another. You jus' setting up a load of trouble." He looked at my cut. "That's better, now."

I stood up. "So why do they do it?"

Thomas finished putting the tools away. "Money," he said. "Always money. You go to town, you see. A free man gets paid for his labour. A slave? They get us to work with chains and whips and barely enough food, then they pile up the money in those big white plantation houses. They don't have to pay us none so they buy themselves horses and carriages and fine, fine clothes. And if we die or starve it ain't no matter to them. They just go to Africa and steal some more of us."

"They don't think we are human?"

Old Thomas laughed. "You ain't learned that much yet?"

We finished clearing up. The sun was setting and the night birds were starting up calling. We set off for our huts on the far side of the hill, out of sight of the big house. Beyond the plantation the hills rose up to the south, and somewhere beyond them Mamma and Martha might be arriving at Mount Vernon, wherever that was.

Our huts, and there were more than I could number on my feet and hands together, stretched out towards the north. Enough for the women and men who worked the sugar cane, the children who worked alongside them in the weeding gangs soon as they could walk, and all the folk who worked in the big house cleaning and washing so the old mistress and young master never had to lift one little finger. There was a whole town's worth of us. All toiling and sweating for those two white folk.

"Why don't we just all wake up, Mr Thomas, in the middle of the night and chase those Barratts off? Move into the big house, live free like the Maroons?"

Old Thomas raised his eyebrows. "You never hear of slave rebellions? Every so often a bunch of us rise up, then they cut us down twice as hard. We kill, or even hurt one white man, they kill twenty of us in return." He let out a long sigh. "Children, women – it ain't nothing to them…"

I kicked a stone off the path. I felt the anger bubbling up inside. "I won't stay here any more, Mr Thomas!"

The old man moved surprisingly fast. He gripped my arm and pulled me around.

"I won't hear no more talk like that! Those woods full of man traps, take your whole leg off. And if you walk along the road, they see your mark, they bring you right back."

I pulled away. I knew he was right, but I kept quiet until we reached the compound where our one-room, mud-built huts were set out around the open-air cookhouse. From the smell of it I reckoned it was roast breadfruit tonight, but I wasn't sure I was hungry. I looked at Mr Thomas.

"You were free once," I said. "What was it like?"

He leaned on his stick. "Coromantee, the west coast of Africa." He smiled a little. "Nicest farm you ever did see, best cattle for miles." His smile faded. "I went out to run an errand for my mother. Last time I saw her I was younger than you are now. I was snatched and

sold and chained up in one of their stinking boats."
He shook his head. "Sometimes I think we only born
to suffer."

I said nothing.

"You thinking about her, son?" Mr Thomas asked.

I was. But I was also thinking about how much I
hated everything in the whole world. Then I saw Bets,
the maid from the big house, come out of our hut,
shaking a mat Mamma had made from rushes and
tossing it aside like it was a piece of dirt. I wanted to
run over and snatch it up, but Thomas put a hand on
my shoulder.

"Time will pass, Nat. Your heart will ease soon
enough."

I didn't want my heart to ease. I wanted to scream
and shout and fetch Mamma back.

"We slaves, we live, we die." Thomas shrugged.
"Maybe when we dead in heaven we get the chance
to be free. . ."

I rubbed at my eyes. They prickled and stung.

I went to line up for supper with the others, but
I could barely eat a mouthful.

So I gave my food to Thomas. Now that the women

had claimed back Mamma's hut, he'd found me space in the hut he shared with the grooms who looked after the horses. Some of the boys from the weeding gangs were catching peenie wallies – fireflies – and maybe last week I'd have gone with them, caught some of my own to put in a bottle, but tonight I couldn't settle to anything.

And when it was time to sleep, I could no more sleep that night than eat. I lay there trying to fix a picture of Mamma and Martha in my mind's eye. But every time I tried to focus on their faces, they just seemed to be getting further and further away.

CHAPTER

3

Three whole months whistled past. The young master spent a lot of his time in Falmouth Town, drinking; or so the kitchen girls told me. I also knew, probably before the young master himself, that his mother had lined up the daughter of an English duke to marry him, whether he liked it or not. From the loud arguments and broken glass and china whenever he came home, I expected he did not.

Despite the young master's rages, a trip to England for the wedding was planned later in the spring.

Betsy and the other house slaves, as well as the butler, the footman and even the drivers, were all on their finest behaviour, hoping they'd be chosen to travel to England with the party. Missis Palmer walked around, as pleased with herself as one of those streamertail hummingbirds, smug that she was definitely going.

One morning, Betsy was told for certain she would not be needed and had a face on her cloudy as hurricane season.

"Why do you want to go to England so much?" I asked her when I brought some soursop and guinep up to the big house.

"Were you born yesterday?" she snapped. "Everybody with half a mind know that there no slaves in England, that the country so good and so perfect none of them English enslaved. I heard you put one foot on the ground and you is free, man, woman or child."

"Is that true?" I put the basket down and Betsy inspected the fruit. She did not look at me.

"Truer than true. England is closer to heaven than anywhere else, and in heaven, we all free."

I was probably the only body on the whole of the Barratt Estate – and there were near a hundred of us – that did not want to jump upon that boat and sail away. But that was because I had plans of my own. Every day while I worked in the kitchen gardens, planting the beans, or raking the soil, thinning the callaloo seedlings, I plotted and planned. Sometimes, when Old Thomas let me, I looked after the pineapples, which were better cared for than any of us. But even then I thought of finding Mamma and Martha. Of being together and being free.

I would wait until the Barratts had gone. Then I would leave in the dead of night, one when the moon was hidden and it was darker than the devil's armpit, down through the cane fields and to the river that bounded the edge of the estate. I would cross the hills that I could see to the south, sleep in the day, maybe up in a tree so no one would find me, and walk at night. If I did get stopped I would say I was running an errand, or something. The important thing was that I would find Mount Vernon – how exactly I was still not certain – but they would be so pleased to see me! And then we'd run, I would carry Martha and

Mamma would run behind us, all the way to the wild mountains of Cockpit Country where the Maroons lived in their hidden town. Free and far from any plantation and any overseer.

I would not spend my life bent and broken like Old Thomas.

One morning, a week before the Barratts were due to set sail, Thomas was tending the young pineapples.

"Come, Nat." He waved me over. "See the leaf? It sharp like a knife. Watch it don't cut you." He moved the leaves out of the way carefully and I could see the pineapple flower, purple and red and spiny. "Hard to think something so ugly taste so sweet," he said. "The pineapple take two years fe' flower, fe' fruit—" He stopped suddenly. For an old man, his ears were sharp, sharp.

It was Missis Palmer, her skirt swishing along the garden path. "Mr Thomas."

She always spoke to him with some respect. Mr Thomas said it was because he knew her mamma. She was wearing her most severe dark blue dress, keys at her waist and hair pulled back.

Old Thomas stood up, took off his hat in a kind of salute. "Missis Palmer."

"They need to take some pineapples. To England. Have them ready by the end of the week."

Thomas shook his head. "Good few months 'til they ready. . ."

She frowned. "That's not good enough. What Mistress Barratt wants. . ."

"Miracles are in short supply around here, Miss P."

"Well, can you not wrap and send plants? Four or five, in the hope that a few will fruit?"

"I hear England is a cold place. Pineapple needs sun. Warmth. Care."

Missis Palmer harrumphed, a sound like the snort of a cow, and swished back into the house.

Old Thomas gave me a wide smile. "Folk can bully folk, but nature will do as she pleases."

Betsy came though the garden later that morning and told us we were wanted in the house after we'd finished our afternoon duties. Thomas scratched his head but said nothing, even though I had never known this happen before. I wanted to ask him what he thought the master or mistress wanted with us but he just sent me over to the far side of the gardens to check on the young sorrel plants. I worried all afternoon that somehow, some way, someone had seen the thoughts inside my head and knew my plans to run away. Perhaps when I was sleeping I had spoken them aloud, or maybe someone had touched me by accident, and my idea to run away had been transmitted through my skin.

When I finally managed to ask him, Thomas had no clue what it was about, which did not reassure me at all.

I imagined the whip, falling hard and fast.

I was not calm when we were shown through the kitchen to Missis Palmer's parlour. This was where she kept her books and inventories. This was where she decided who of the household slaves were sold or moved on to the field.

Then I saw old Mistress Barratt, sitting in Missis Palmer's armchair, skirts spread out so that it looked as if she had no legs, her hand resting on her polished hardwood stick as if she were some kind of queen. Which I suppose she was. Mr Bird walked across Missis Palmer's desk, and I could see Missis

Palmer curl her lip a little. No one liked that creature save the old mistress. I kept my hands behind my back and prayed that green-feathered monster didn't come any closer. I reached up and rubbed the back of my head where I had felt the blow of that stick last, thinking the worst. Somehow, they knew I wanted to run away. I looked down at my bare feet, dull with mud.

"Thomas, Miss Palmer here has told me that there are no fruits on the pineapples."

I felt my whole body relax. This was about fruit, not escape.

"Yess'm, Missis." Thomas spoke in a low monotone, kept his own eyes fixed down – not the way he spoke to me in the garden. In fact he sounded as if he too was a twelve-year-old boy. This, I knew, was the way you had to speak to white people. If they thought you were simple they were less likely to hit you.

"We are sailing on Friday. I wish to take some fruit, or failing that some plants."

Mr Bird skipped back to the old mistress's shoulder. She fed it a grape, and Mr Bird held it in its claw and I saw its tongue, black and wizened.

Thomas shifted a little; I knew it was hard for him to stand still for long with only half a foot.

Mistress Barratt went on. "Miss Palmer has reminded me that pineapples are not a natural fit with the English climate."

"No'm, Missis."

Mistress Barrett thumped her stick hard on the ground. Mr Bird flew up, flapped and screeched. Thomas and I fairly jumped.

"Thomas, is your skull as empty as a glutton's dinner plate?"

"No'm, Missis."

The stick thumped again and Mr Bird screeched. "I have promised pineapples to the Duke of Mistleton and his wife. And I shall have them. Pack up the plants in readiness for the boat."

She got up. Thomas and I stepped back instinctively.

Missis Palmer coughed a little. Dipped a curtsey. "Thomas said the plants will need care and attention. On the journey, ma'am."

Mistress Barratt looked from her to Thomas, and finally to me. I could feel her stone-grey eyes boring into me for the longest time. Outside the wind rattled through the palm trees.

"Then the boy can attend them."

I looked up. She had gone.

"I can't!" I hissed to Thomas as Missis Palmer shooed us out. He shushed me and I held my tongue until we were back in the garden.

"I cannot go to England!" I wailed. "I will not go! I will not!"

Thomas slapped me across the face. I was stunned with shock.

"Don't you realize how lucky you are, Nathaniel Barratt? You stop moaning and moping right now."

I sniffed. "But I promised I'd find Mamma and—"

"Think! She would want this too! She would want you to tek this chance in both your hands. Freedom!" He took me by the shoulders. "She and the pickney, they will manage without you."

"I'll never see them again." I couldn't help shuddering.

Thomas's voice was steady. "Listen. We all lost people. We all lost everyone. That's how they mek us live, like we cattle." I looked at him. "Nathaniel, you pack up those plants and you tek yourself forward. Imagine – this is your chance to hold your head up."

He patted my shoulder, ran his hand across my head.

"Come, Nat. We have a look for some wood. And maybe some glass. Those plants need protection. Like a lot of living things I don't know if they'll survive the salt sea."

I was still a bit wobbly. All those plans I'd made. . . But then maybe I could change those plans. It might take longer but perhaps Thomas was right. Maybe I could be free and make my fortune and come back and save Mamma and Martha. I ran to catch Thomas up. He was already heading down the garden path towards the tool shed.

"How long," I called, "does it take to sail to England?"

As the days passed I began to make new plans. Perhaps London was paved with gold like Bets in the kitchen said. I asked Thomas over and over about it and he told me that he doubted anywhere in the world was paved with anything but poor folks' troubles. He said all he knew was that London was cold and that the rain that fell was also cold. Even if it wasn't paved with actual gold, there were so many rich people all in one place, I thought there was a good chance some of them would drop money and forget to pick it up.

On the last morning before the boat set sail, we packed up the pineapple plants and carried them to the wagon. I had helped make the boxes, one for each plant, with sliding glass lids.

"See?" Old Thomas said as we loaded them up. "These little plants have nice, nice likkle homes. Give them plenty of air and keep them warm if the weather turn, yuh hear?"

I nodded. I looked at him and thought to myself that here was another face I would have to keep a hold of in my mind.

"You keep your head up, Nat."

"You're not coming down to the ship?" I said. "See me off?"

He shook his head. "Can't say as me and ships get along. That one journey was enough for me."

I nodded. Old Thomas reached out and flattened my hair. "Your hair stick up so…"

I didn't pull away.

"You a fine boy," he said. "Your mamma be proud, proud." He coughed a little, leaned close. "You go to Englan', Nat. You be free!"

It felt like there was something hard stuck in my throat and I could not speak. I turned away and climbed up into the wagon, and watched until we turned the corner and I couldn't see him or Barratt Hall any more.

I was surprised at how my heart leaped when at last the wagon rolled down the hill into port and I saw thirty or more massive sailing ships, masts striking up into the sky. Even though I felt a deep sadness at leaving Thomas and home, there was excitement rising up in my chest and I could not stop it. Beside me the boxes we'd made, all of them with sliding glass lids, clanked and rattled along. I was going to England. I would be free.

The houses in Falmouth were new and dripped money, and my eyes fairly popped out seeing even brown-skinned folk wearing good coats and hats. There were traders from everywhere. Watching so many busy people I realized I knew nothing about towns or cities – and wasn't London the biggest city on earth? How big would that city be? Twice as big as this one? Four times?

We turned a corner and passed a market: women selling yam, mango and banana, cloth and all sorts of fixings. Then we rolled through another open space and there were sharp-looking white men, some red-faced, some with straw hats, most with short canes tucked under their arms – selling something else. They stood naked and chained: rows of men, women and children. All around, the smell of death and the sound of soft sad whimpering. A boy just old enough to walk was holding his mother's hand, crying and crying as his mother was prodded like a prize cow. Her eyes were full of fear and despair.

I wanted to do something, stop it, stop them all, put an arrow into every one of those men's hearts. I felt myself shaking. I was powerless.

The wagon rolled on, past the marketplace towards the docks.

I spied the young master on the dockside, his breeches so white they shone, his boots so glossy a man could see his face in them. And there was the old mistress with him, wearing her best bonnet, her face as hard and cold as a stone from the river. Their faces wore the same expressions as those monsters I had seen in the slave market. And I would have to spend weeks with them in a floating wooden world.

Mr Bird was in a cage, flapping and squawking. The old mistress put some cloth over the cage, which quietened him. I reckoned he was as unhappy to have left the estate as I was. But Mr Bird and the old mistress were said to be the same age, and neither one could leave the other.

The wagon pulled to a stop. I made sure not to meet their gaze as I helped unload the plant boxes with some of the sailors, but the young master noticed me and swaggered across the quayside, face sour as turned milk.

"These are the pineapples?"

The sailors said nothing. I nodded.

"And you are the boy. Well, I hope you know your work." He leaned down, closer, smiling like a snake about to strike. "Remember, boy, if these plants die, I will get these sailors to throw you overboard – for the sharks…"

CHAPTER

4

The ship was called *The Brave Venture*. It had three masts and what seemed to me at first like a thousand sails. In time I learned there were fifteen.

And I was not thrown overboard. Although there were times, weeks into the crossing, when the sea rolled and rolled and I swore I would rather die then than live through the storm.

The Barratts kept to their cabin mostly, and Mr Bird stayed in his cage, as the old mistress was worried he might be lost at sea. I made sure to keep out of their way. I noticed they didn't have much luggage, only one trunk each. Missis Palmer told me they planned on buying fine English goods for their return, as clothes in England were much better quality than anything you could buy on the island. I said nothing, but noted that the old mistress seemed to have left her stick behind at Barratt Hall and gave thanks.

I learned a lot. The sailors were, like those in the town of Falmouth, men of all colours from across the world, and unlike us slaves, all of them were paid for their labour. I got used to looking some of the white sailors in the eyes when we spoke, especially the mate, Mr Kelsall, who seemed like the saddest man I ever met. He kept me busy with various errands and chores, and it pleased me to think that even though I was a slave I was not kept chained up as Thomas said they were on the journey from Africa.

And some of the crew even spoke to me as an equal: Ivan the cook, who came from somewhere so far north, he said the sea froze solid half the year (I did not believe him) and Georges a deckhand from Brazil. Then there was the cabin boy, Henry, who looked half my age even though he swore blind he was fourteen, and so older than me by a couple of years. I was surprised when he first sat down beside me, to eat his midday meal.

"In London," he explained, "where I am from, there are all sorts of folk."

I made sure to seek him out when I had any time between chores.

I envied Henry's ease at sea. I watched him climb a rope faster than a rat up a tree and he capered helter-skelter along the yardarm of the main mast as if he were on solid ground. My heart was in my mouth.

When he came down he was laughing at me. "Your face! You were scared!"

"Was not," I lied. "Back home on the estate, I have shinned up palm trees just as fast as you!" I looked him straight in the face then because that bit, at least, was the truth. And I realized it was the very first time I had stared down a white boy. I stared harder. I would not give way.

Henry shook his head and smiled. "Come up then!" he said. "Come up, Nat, and see. You can look upon the edge of the world. There's nothing like it." He took the rope in his hand. I had not moved. "You are scared!"

"No," I protested. "I'm not!"

So up I went after him. And even though he tried to frighten me by making the rope swing and sway, I found it an easy climb. Narrower than a tree trunk, but with plenty of grip to it. I was up before I thought about what I was doing or where I was going. But when I inched over on to the yardarm, the narrow wooden pole from which hung the main mast, and saw the world of water far below reeling and rolling. I felt cold and sick with fear.

Henry did not seem to notice my unease, only shifted himself along the yardarm.

"Look!" He pointed out behind the ship. "Dolphins!"

Henry was sitting on the spar as comfortably as the young master would sit in the deep-sided wicker chair on the veranda at Barratt Hall. I pulled myself into a sitting position beside him. I felt my legs hanging down, loose in the air, and the long nothingness that stretched out underneath. My stomach turned over and I held on tight.

"Nat, see?" he said, pointing.

I was gripping the spar I sat on so tightly that

my knuckles showed white through my skin. Henry elbowed me and I thought for a moment that I would fall.

I cannot remember how I made it down, only that I never went up there again and I kept my feet firmly on the deck, even when Henry told me I was missing an unusual cloud formation or school of flying fish. And to be fair Henry did not laugh, he said I had done well for a landlubber – the name for those, like me, who preferred dry land.

One morning when we were scrubbing the deck I decided to share my story. "You have to promise me, Henry, you won't tell a soul. If the Barratts find out. . ." I drew my finger across my throat as if I was cutting it.

Henry spat on his palm and put it out for me to shake. "I'd never rat on you! Don't you know that?" He looked at me with a serious expression, and I could see he was sad I didn't trust him. I glanced round the deck and checked none of the other crew were near. Then I shook his hand hard and told him about my life on the plantation, about Mamma and Martha, and how I planned to return to Jamaica and free my family.

He said it was a fine thing I was doing, and told me about himself.

"I grew up in London," he began. "An innkeeper's son. I ran to sea after my brother Jacob, who was pressed."

"Pressed? What's that?"

He stopped. "Have you not heard of the press gang?"

I shook my head.

"They take men for the navy. By force."

"Like slavery?" I asked.

Henry shook his head. "Oh, there's payment," he said. "But no choice. My brother Jacob was tricked into taking the King's shilling. He was right sore, but I being only ten years old and having no more wits than an empty cup, went after him of my own accord, thinking to keep him company."

Henry told me a merchant ship such as this was a million times better than a navy man o'war he'd been on at first. He said he'd had enough of the Spanish wars and planned to work his way up to mate and make his old man proud.

I told him I was going to London to seek my freedom and he wished me luck.

"I've seen those slave ships, smelled their foul stink," he said. "And I've seen the schools of sharks following, waiting for an easy meal. I cannot imagine a worse sort of life."

We picked up the bucket of dirty water and carried it to the side of the boat. Mr Kelsall the mate was busy close by, looking over some sails for mending.

Henry and I lifted up the heavy pail and slopped it over the side. The sea swirled green and blue alongside the boat and looking down into it I swallowed, anxious.

"So they do really throw folk to the sharks? Alive?" I said.

Mr Kelsall looked up when he heard me. "Oh yes. Those sharks don't follow the ships for nothing. Some Africans try to throw themselves overboard rather than live in chains. Think when they are dead they will float up into the sky and fly back to Africa." He shook his head.

"Is this your story again, Mr Kelsall? About the massacre?" Henry said, and nudged me, whispered low. "He would marry my sister, Nancy, and has told her so many tales, all of them sad."

Mr Kelsall looked hurt. "Would that it were only a story..."

"Mr Kelsall worked the trade," Henry said. "The slave trade."

I shuddered. I had heard stories too: men, women and children chained and packed like fish in a barrel.

The mate nodded. "Never again. Things I've seen would make a grown man lose his reason. I've seen men turn into monsters on account of money."

Henry picked up the empty bucket and his mop but I stopped. I looked at Mr Kelsall. His face was brown with weather and sun and his eyes had almost the same sadness I'd seen in Old Thomas's.

"What did you see?" I asked.

"You heard of the Middle Passage?" he said.

I nodded. Henry did too.

"We load up in Liverpool with blankets and buttons, brass goods that shine but cost tuppence to make, then sail to the coast of Africa, buy up as many Africans as we can cram into the hold and sail west."

"Why do you pack us so tight?" I said. "It never made sense to me, so many die on the boats..."

Mr Kelsall shook his head. "The more Africans we carry, the more we sell. If a few die, ten or twenty even, we still make a good bounty."

"But the chains?" Henry asked. "Why chain the poor souls up?"

I said nothing. I was furious just thinking about it.

"We need the chains. Sometimes there's only small crew, twenty men or so, and on my last voyage on the *Zong*, up to four hundred slaves. If they weren't in chains, and we never had guns, they'd kill us all."

"I can see that," Henry said.

I was still fuming. Mr Kelsall went on.

"And we have to season them up, get them used to the hard life that's coming. Make them realize they aren't people any more. Just goods."

I stood up, ready to walk away. If I didn't leave, I would punch something.

Mr Kelsall stopped me. "I know. I understand it all now – the cruelty, the pain. I will never forget. You do not know how hard the memories press down on my soul." His eyes were pale and watery.

"I deserve your hatred," he said. "What I saw on that last voyage, no man should ever see." He breathed in a long shuddering breath. "People tossed overboard. The bodies in the water, all those sharks thrashing beneath, turning the sea red." He blinked a tear. "Those poor souls."

Mr Kelsall mumbled to himself and made the sign of the cross.

"How is that possible?" I said, fury burning in my heart.

The mate blinked at me, then hurried away. He wiped a tear as he went. I had never seen a grown white man shed tears and I longed to follow him and ask him more. But I had promised to help Henry and we still had plenty of work to finish.

"Did you see that?" I asked him when Mr Kelsall had gone below deck. "Those tears?"

Henry shrugged. "That voyage he talked about, that was a year or two ago at least, a ship called the *Zong*. He thought to make his fortune, but since he returned – and poor as he set out – he's been that melancholy. Except if you get him talking about our Nancy. Oh he's a good heart, and I do believe that's his problem."

"No man should buy or sell another," I said. "It is an evil trade."

"True enough." Henry picked up the empty pail. "I know there's many of us would rather fight the French or the Spanish – or both – than crew a slave ship." Henry frowned. "I can't imagine what it would be like to be bought and sold like meat or cattle." He shook his head. "I would not wish that on my worst enemy, and you are, I think, my friend."

I smiled. I had never had a white friend.

"Henry?" I asked. "I have heard that in England there are no slaves at all. That slavery is not allowed..."

Henry shrugged. "My family, well my sister Nancy mostly, runs a pub, The Cat and Mutton, down by the docks in Shadwell. I've seen folk of all colours in there, sailors, servants ... can't recall seeing any slaves as such."

I took some comfort in Henry's shrug. Even though I looked for Mr Kelsall later I did not find him, and from that day on the mate avoided me. He looked away when I greeted him – he seemed afraid that I might ask him more.

We suffered one more storm, in cold northern waters, when the boat rolled and rocked so hard I carried all my pineapple plants, snug in their boxes, down into the space under my hammock, where, along with everything else, they slid backwards and forwards as we were tossed on the waves. In the turmoil the glass broke on one of the boxes and I was forced to repot the plant, soil and all, up close with another.

But the young master and the old mistress were both too sick to notice and we sailed into the Port of London seven weeks after leaving Jamaica.

Henry said farewell on the dockside.

"Not goodbye though," he said, hugging me. "We will meet again, I know it. When I am master of my own ship."

"I worry that may be too long."

"Perhaps. Tell you what," Henry said as he helped me load up the last of the pineapple boxes. Missis Palmer watched, from a distance. She looked damp and cold. Henry lowered his voice. "Since you're free now, why don't you tell old sourface to stuff it?"

"Hurry, boy!" she called. I looked at her. Was I free now? Maybe I didn't have to go anywhere.

I didn't move. Could I really talk back to Missis Palmer?

"Don't forget!" Henry said. "The Cat and Mutton. If I'm not there, ask for Nancy. I'll be staying there 'til I get a new ship. I expect Mr Kelsall will be sniffing around too. But don't let that put you off. You make a better brother than I've ever had."

I blinked. Had he really said that? He saluted, pulled his bag on to his shoulder, and made his way off the dock.

"Nathaniel!" Missis Palmer's voice cut the air like a knife. Suddenly she was there beside me and twisted my ear hard.

"Owwww!"

"Those who cannot hear must feel!" she said, and marched me towards the front of the cart.

I climbed up into the cart behind Missis Palmer. She threw me such a look but I didn't care. I had a friend and a brother. And I was in London.

The city was filthy. It was May and the moon was high in the sky, shining brightly. But every building, even those fine ones, taller than mountains, seemed to be very dark. But I did not care. I breathed in deep.

Was this what freedom felt like?

The streets were crowded, the like of which I had never seen: animals, men and women, and running between the crowds what seemed like an army of children, unshod and clothed in rags. I had imagined London, the grandest city in the whole of the world, to be, if not quite paved with gold, then perhaps wearing its good fortune, instead of hiding its wealth under a cloak of soot and grime.

As the cart slowed up behind what I guessed was the Barratts' London house, I shut my eyes and made a promise to myself. I would unpack the pineapples, safe in their boxes, settle them into their new home in English soil. And then I would ask the old mistress for my freedom.

No, not ask, I would demand it.

CHAPTER

5

LONDON

I had to help unload the Barratts' trunks as we arrived early. There were two footmen at the door with white powdered wigs who looked down their long noses at me as I struggled inside. I reckoned they had been dragged out of their beds to welcome the Barratts, as their jackets were not fastened and their boots still unbuttoned.

I must say I had never seen anything like that

house. Barratt Hall in Jamaica was large and fine, but mostly made of wood. This house had a hall that was floored with black-and-white tiles, and a huge staircase that curved round and up as far as I could see. There were so many candles, their flames reflected in so many bright shining mirrors, that even though it was dark outside it seemed like daylight indoors. My mouth must have fallen open, as Missis Palmer told me to leave the trunk at the bottom of the steps and find the servants' staircase instead.

It was late when at last Missis Palmer showed me my bed. Only it was not a bed, rather a straw mattress laid out under a table in the kitchen. Not the bed of a free man, I thought, but I was too tired to argue, and my legs still not used to solid ground after being on board ship for so long. I lay down but could not sleep. I twisted and turned, wondering if Mamma knew I was so far away, and how long it would take me before I could step off the boat at Falmouth a free man, a pocket full of English money, ready to buy her and Martha's freedom. Three months? Before the winter came? If I took a year Martha could be walking and talking and sold away before I got back.

I prayed hard until I slept. When I woke up I reminded myself that praying had never done me nor anyone else I knew any good and opened my eyes. As the room was in the basement of the house I could look up out of the window and see feet passing above, boots and buckles, black and brown leather, even a pair of unshod feet, pale as milk. Were there really poor white folk in this famous city?

The floor was hard and in the early light it was cool. I lay still, worrying about the morning – about standing up to the old mistress, and claiming my freedom – but also about the plants outside. Were they too cold? I thought I might drift off in the dawn but the next thing I knew the household began to wake up around me.

A girl came in: small, with shiny brown hair the colour of polished wood. She was wearing a blue shawl, her skirt pinned up so it didn't drag on the floor. She began to sweep out the ashes, and as she worked she sang. It was a song I'd never heard before, about a girl wrapped in a sheepskin or some such stupidness.

Then from outside there was another noise, a

low rumbling like far-off thunder. I forgot about the pineapples and got up, wanting to see.

"God's own mercy!" The girl jumped a mile. She turned on me, brush held out like a weapon. Then she paused, studied me. "Are you with Mr Shadrack?" She put the broom down. "Do you dance too?"

"No!" I was affronted, but did my best to cover it. I had scared her and now felt stupid myself. I put my hands up. "Sorry, miss. I came with the Barratts." I bowed. "I am Nathaniel, from Jamaica, come to look after the pineapples."

"Of course! I clean forgot." She smiled and bobbed a curtsey. "Mary Lee. From Hackney." She must have seen the look on my face as I had never heard of the place. "It is a village on the edge of London. My family are gardeners too."

"I only wanted to see the street," I told her. "I've never been to London and we arrived last night, very late."

"Good morning then, Nathaniel. Although I think I shall call you Nat if you don't mind as that involves a good deal less letters." She put down the pan full of ashes and wiped her hands on her apron. "There is an easier way. Here, out through the front area."

I hesitated.

"We're not going far," she said. "And Cook's not up yet. Come on."

Mary opened a door that led to a basement courtyard with steps leading up. The light was so different from home, softer, I thought. The sky was blue but pale as if it were further away. I held back, but she took my hand and led me up to the street and out through the black-painted railings that bordered the house.

The house lay set back from the main road, one of a sort of curtain of tall houses that I later learned was a terrace, all painted white and set around a patch of green grass, which was the square garden. There were no verandas and the trees were all small and new-looking, with bright green new leaves. None would bear climbing. And I saw straight away that the ground was paved with nothing but stone.

What was truly astounding, though, was the noise. It was not thunder. From the main road to the south, the sound of many horses, a thousand iron hooves and wheels trundling over the granite road. And so many people singing their wares: watercress, roses, a man offering to sharpen knives.

"Sometimes on a Sunday there's a puppet show for the little ones in the park, and, oh! You must have heard of him. Mr Shadrack Furman? Darker skinned than you, dances lovely. He is so clever! He has this model ship as a hat and the dance makes it seem like it's rolling on an ocean."

I stopped listening. I had had my fill of oceans and boats. In the middle of the square, I noticed a milkmaid all in white sitting on a small stool beside the filthiest cow I ever saw.

"Are you catching flies?" Mary was grinning. "Only your cakehole is so wide open I swear you could drive a coach and horses right down it!"

Over the noise came a louder, higher yell from behind us. The smile dropped from Mary's face. She gasped.

"Quick!" she said, and ran back down the steps.

I followed reluctantly, and found Mary, hands over her head, being set about by a woman wearing an apron, who I guessed must be Cook.

"Stop!" I stepped in between Cook and Mary, and received the back of Cook's hand for my trouble. "There is no slavery here! This is England!"

Cook froze, hand in mid-air. Mary gave me a look that was far from grateful.

Cook looked at me. "Slavery? Mary Muggins here gets paid over six pounds a year and gets every Sunday afternoon off! For six pounds a year I reckon as I can hit her as often as I like."

Six pounds a year, I thought. A grown field slave like Mamma sold for forty or fifty pounds. I would need to work hard to earn enough money for Mamma and Martha.

Mary picked up the broom and began sweeping like her life depended on it. "My name is not Muggins."

"Your name's what I say it is." Cook picked up a poker from the fireside. I thought she might do Mary an injury but she merely riddled the fire with it. "'Specially when you're gallivanting round the garden square like you own the place when I've so much work for you to do. Have you forgotten the duke and his family arrive at the end of the week? We have to impress him and his daughter. So your man can take her home to Jamaica."

Mary kept sweeping and said nothing. I was reminded of my own situation. Still, she was beaten and paid. She could walk out of this house and into another with every part of her feet still attached to her legs.

Cook studied her hand where she'd hit me. "You're the black boy? Doesn't come off does it?" She laughed at this ignorant comment as if she had made a most excellent joke.

"I swear you look nearer brown than black. I hope you don't turn the milk with that sour face." She began to roll up her sleeves. "Your Missis Palmer, her with a broomstick up her fundament, she says I'm to tell you to see to the piney apples." Cook wiped the tabletop with one hand and emptied some flour on to it with the other. "I think she's worried the house cat has done its business among them, or will do if they're left out in the garden any longer. And the upstairs maids are all in a fluster with that blessed parrot snapping its great beak at them. It's not natural if you ask me..."

She shooed me out towards the garden before I could attempt to question her further. I went quickly, just in case she picked up the poker again and decided to use it on me.

The back garden was smaller than the garden square and surrounded by a high brick wall. There were so many roses, climbing up and around the walls just like the ones back in Barratt Hall, their scent took my breath away. Save for the roses, there was a square lawn with a summer house in the centre, surrounded by low shrubs. The backs of the other tall houses rose up like a curtain of bricks. Higher still, were small dots of birds, swooping and calling up in the sky.

Banging on the window brought me back down to earth. I looked up at the house and saw Missis Palmer giving me the evil eye from the first floor. She indicated that I should wait. A moment later she came out into the garden, showing me the glasshouse, which leaned up against the back wall. By the smell of the fresh sawn wood, it had been newly built.

Inside, the pineapples were in their boxes on the ground. One look told me they would need more heat than this pale English sun. I thought of what Thomas would do. Before I left, he had told me that piled-up hay could create its own kind of heat. I told Missis Palmer what I needed and she directed me to the mews behind the house, where the household kept their horses and carriages.

"There is a door at the far end of the garden, you will find what you need there," she said. I started off towards it but she called out, "Nathaniel! This is not home. There is to be no more wandering around the streets. Cook told me what happened this morning."

I almost went to speak, to explain myself, but stopped. She would not listen. Nothing I said mattered. She went on.

"You are only here to work in the garden or the kitchen. You're not to go upstairs without permission. You must remember who you are!"

I looked at the ground. As if I could forget, I thought, and went to find the door. It was stiff and hard to open, but I slipped out into what seemed like another world.

There was so much activity and industry. The stables served all the large houses in the square. At the end of the mews was a blacksmith's forge where a man was shoeing the finest dapple-grey horse I had ever seen, its mane shining like silver silk. I thought then it must be the truth; that everything English was indeed superior. Then I came upon a swarm of men mending a cart whose axle had been snapped in two, by the looks of it. I could have stayed there all day and watched. And what's more, nobody gave me a second glance. I had imagined that, this being England, and darker skins being rare, folks would stare. But none of this army of working men gave me so much as a second look. Indeed, the groom, who could have been only a couple of years older than me, was polite as a gentleman, simply asking how much hay I needed and supplying me with a wheelbarrow.

When I returned, Missis Palmer came back to the garden and stood watching me as I piled the hay around the plants.

"Will they live?" she asked. "The regular gardener Mr French says he won't have anything to do with them."

I wheeled my barrow to a halt. "I am doing all I can, Missis Palmer, but I must admit they are suffering."

"They need to look their best." She frowned and looked at me as if I was no more than a piece of dirt. But that was her normal manner of looking, so what she said next was rather a surprise.

"You will see to the fruit and then come with me. You need a decent set of clothes. The Barratts have decided to make a present of you to the duke and duchess along with the plants."

My mouth must have dropped open.

"They have a fondness for the exotic, otherwise I cannot think why anyone would consider you a gift."

"A gift? Missis Palmer, I have done my duty..."

She looked at me and I could not fathom her expression, not disgust, not disdain.

"Duty?"

"Yes," I said. I had not meant to bring up the matter of my freedom with Missis Palmer, but perhaps this was the time.

"You will do as you are told. You have no duty. You belong to the Barratts and soon you will belong to the Duke and Duchess of Mistleton."

I shook my head. "Oh no! Missis Palmer you do not understand. We are in England now. I am free. I will tell the mistress and young master and—"

Missis Palmer burst out laughing. She put her hand over her mouth so I didn't have to look at her gnarly teeth, but she laughed and laughed. Eventually she composed herself.

"Free? Hah! And I am the King of England's mother!"

She turned on her heel and went back inside the house.

"There will be no more embarrassing yourself or the Barratts with talk of freedom! You are property. We all are. And you, Nathaniel Barratt, will be a slave until the day you die!"

I felt a little shaky, but knew I was in the right. Clearly Missis Palmer was just trying to upset me, or else didn't have her facts straight. I piled up the hay to keep the plants warm, as if I was tucking them up in a sick bed. I saw my plans turning to dust. I went back inside to find Mary Lee washing pots. Cook was nowhere to be seen.

"Mary Lee?" I asked. "Are there slaves here in England? Bought and sold like dogs or carpets or fruit?"

She nodded, matter of fact. "Course."

I felt my stomach drop. There was a knot in my throat so big I could barely swallow.

"Are they only black like me?"

"Naturally." She dried her hands on her apron and went to the table where there was a tray with the remains of what I recognized as the young master's breakfast and a newspaper, folded in half. Mary unfolded it.

"Look. Notices for slaves that have run away from their owners. Every week there are three or four." She jabbed her finger at the squiggly lines I knew were words but could not make out. None of us back home could. In fact I remembered Mamma had been beaten, more than once, for trying to learn her letters.

Mary continued. "And here, a sale of slaves at…" She peered close. "Long Acre, that's a street in Covent Garden, that is."

She pushed the paper towards me but the letters meant nothing.

"How can you tell, you are a kitchen maid."

She looked at me, cracked a broad smile. "You cannot read!"

"And you can?"

Mary nodded. "Sunday school at the Methodist chapel. It came naturally, not like scrubbing or sweeping. But there was only the Bible. Here in town there are no end of words, on bills posted up in the street and newspapers and such like." She shrugged. "But as Cook says, words en't no use in a kitchen."

She smoothed out the paper. "It says here, two boys are for sale in town this very week. And from the look of notices, like this one –" she pointed at the newspaper – "that if you run away folk will track you down."

I felt cold. "Are you inventing this? How do I know what you say is true?"

Mary snorted "What reason do I have to lie!" She picked up the paper. "I will read," she said, "since you cannot." I looked away a little ashamed. She cleared her throat. "*Runaway from a house in Hanover Square – Cuffay, grey livery, black cap. Hair cut short. Speaks English, Dutch and African. Anyone who returns him to Mr Harris at the following address shall receive a reward.* There. And another one. *Boy, around nine years old, runaway from a house in St James –* that's near here – *wearing a silver collar with his name 'Toby' and address written on it. Reward promised for finder.*"

"No!" I cried out. "I was sure there was no slavery here. We all knew that. I had planned to make my fortune before I returned. I thought in England everyone was free." My mind was racing. "Those boys? When they find them will they cut off their feet?"

Mary goggled. "Pardon?"

"Cut off your foot so you can't run away again? Or slit their noses?"

Mary looked indignant. "That is horrible!"

"They don't do that here, then?" I asked. "Do they?"

"Some places they still lock you up in the stocks and folk pelt you with eggs or mouldy cabbages." She stopped to think. "Oh, there's whippings surely, hangings, brandings sometimes. . ."

"Only sometimes?" I said. "All of us the Barratts own have this." I pulled at the collar of my shirt to show the B pressed into my skin by a hot iron.

Mary gasped. "God in Glory! They treat you worse than a dog! Did they take your finger too?"

"That was Mr Bird, the parrot."

"It did that?" She paused. "Even so, I should like to see it! Only I'm not allowed in the house, not unless Maggie is ill and I have to lay the fires and clean out the ashes. Maggie says he is green and red and one hundred years old. She says she is afraid of him and he bit one of the footmen. . ."

I was about to tell her why Maggie was right to be scared when Cook slammed in from the pantry, I rearranged my shirt and Mary began drying the dishes as if her life depended on it.

Cook nodded at me. "Your Missis Palmer wants you right away, boy. I hear you're to have a new suit of clothes, and maybe shoes too! You're a lucky fellow. What I'd give for some new shoes. . ."

Missis Palmer had her office next to the kitchen. She was standing at the small table with a gentleman wearing an inch measure around his neck and a small pair of glasses on his nose. A jacket was laid out on the table, sewn all over with flowers and fruit. It was so brightly coloured anyone would see the wearer from a mile away. Missis Palmer lifted it up gently, clucking with approval.

"Nathanial Barratt, in England even a slave may dress like a prince." She saw me and her face fell. "Get that hay out of your hair, boy!"

I patted my hair clean but said nothing about the coat. I thought any prince wearing that would look as if something had been sick all over them.

"Such fine needlework!" Missis Palmer went on, and the tailor blushed.

"Put it on then, put it on!" She held it up and I could see it was meant for someone smaller, but still she hustled me into it. It weighed a ton and it was too tight. I could barely lift my arms.

"How will I work wearing this?" I said.

"Be quiet, boy!" Missis Palmer snapped at me. She nodded. "This fit will do."

The tailor smiled. I started to take it off when Mississ Palmer held up her hand to stop me. Then she brought out what I thought at first was a cushion, but then realized was a bright red silken hat. "Your turban!"

She squashed it down upon my head and smiled. "There!"

It took every ounce of strength not to tear the thing off my head.

"The outfit will definitely need a hat," the tailor said. "I have heard it's mighty cold up in Mistleton.

Up north, it is, Yorkshire way. . ."

I swallowed. I wanted to ask how far north.

Missis Palmer cut in, "You will attend the mistress tomorrow. Make sure you are clean and there is no hay in your hair."

I looked at the ground. I wanted so much to run out of that house, but I thought of those notices in the newspaper. Even if I managed to run away, I still needed somewhere safe to go. Perhaps I could get Mary to write to Henry's sister at the inn?

"Oh!" Missis Palmer exclaimed. "The shoes! The shoes!"

She bought out a pair of silver-buckled shoes made of the same stuff as the jacket. I would look like a junkanoo carnival dancer. At least nobody from home was here to see me. The cane-field boys would have laughed themselves sick.

"Tomorrow we will begin teaching you how to pour tea," she said, and shooed me out of her office and shut the door.

I went into the garden then, behind the glasshouse where no one from the house could see, and kicked at stones. My blood felt hot as anger bubbled and burned under my skin. I would not be a dressed-up clown for any duke! I would not go to Mistleton. I would be free. I would find Henry, and perhaps his sister would let me work at the inn. Or perhaps he'd know someone who would find me work.

I had promises to keep.

After working in the garden I found Mary in the kitchen washing dishes. When I told her about the clothes she laughed. And then I laughed too; the thought of me in that stupid outfit pouring tea for a duke and duchess was indeed a funny one. Mary had a huge pile of dishes to get through so I lent a hand, taking the kettle of hot water off the fire and pouring it into the sink.

"My brother Joshua would say it's not worth letting the lords and nabobs get the better of you."

"The gardener?" I cut in. "I should like to meet him."

"I do think you two would get along. It is indeed a shame you won't be staying in London."

I took up a clean cloth and began to dry the dishes. I smiled, thinking that perhaps, with Henry's help, I would.

Next morning I woke before dawn to the sound of clattering and banging. For a moment I was terrified, imagining something had happened to Mamma or Thomas. But it was Mary, sitting on the kitchen floor and opening cupboard doors, rummaging through each of them in turn. The stub of a candle rested on the table, flickering in the dark. I sat up and rubbed my eyes.

"Mary?"

She pulled out a bucket and a broom from a small cupboard and took a pile of rags from a shelf, and tucked them under her arm.

"Are you all right?" I said, getting up from my bed.

"It's nothing." She stood up, picking up the candle. "I've work to do." Her face was grey with ashes.

"What's happened? Let me help."

She bit her lip, put down the candle and rubbed her eyes. I could see she was almost in tears. "I never meant it to happen, I was doing the fires for Maggie, I just wanted a look at Mr Bird. I've made an awful mess!"

I went with her upstairs – after all, four hands would clean up faster than two. She opened the door from the servants' staircase to the first floor, and led me across the landing through a set of double doors. In the yellow candlelight I could see the room was huge, big as a field, with curtained windows and walls lined with books. Chairs were set around the fireplace at one end, and I could see the familiar shape of Mr Bird's cage, covered for the night with a cloth.

"I had swept up, Nat, see?" Mary was saying as we crept inside. "Then I thought I'd take a look at that parrot." Mary kept her voice low and pointed at the cage. "I only lifted a corner of that cloth, and he was there asleep, head tucked under his wing, like nothing more than a dove." She paused, looked at me. "Then he woke up."

I could imagine her shock.

"Oh!" she whispered. "I dropped that cloth sharp!"

"You were lucky no one heard," I said. "His screech can wake the dead."

Mary nodded miserably. "Then I tried to stop the bucket crashing, and I managed that, but it fell on to the carpet and rolled away." She held up the candle and showed the damage: there was a pile of ash in front of the fire and all over the pale green rug. "We'll never get it clean before they wake!"

"Of course we will," I said, but I wasn't sure if I was right.

I took the brush she'd bought from downstairs and began sweeping.

Mary explained she couldn't manage if they cut her wages.

"But couldn't you find another job? You're free, aren't you?" I said.

"Not without a good reference."

I swept harder. Outside it was getting light, and the stub of candle had burned down into a pool of wax.

I went to the window, taking care to go quietly round the birdcage, and opened the curtains and shutters to let in some light. The rug was still a little grey, but the fireplace was clean again. Mary pushed the hair away from her face. She almost smiled. "Nearly there."

"If we could give that rug a beat—" I began.

We both froze, looking at each other. Mary's face went pale. We could hear someone outside.

"Quick!" We put the bucket of ash and the brushes in the grate. I pulled her towards the window and pushed her behind the curtain just as the door opened. Missis Palmer didn't see me at first. She strode straight to the birdcage and lifted it up without removing the cloth. Then she stopped.

"Nathaniel Barratt!" She spat my name as if it was the worst curse in the world. "What are you doing upstairs?" She put the cage down, spotting the grey cast to the rug. "This is your doing?"

I tried to think of something clever to say, but all I could see were Mary Lee's two feet poking out from under the curtain. I looked away from them and into Missis Palmer's face as she bore down on me.

"I'm sorry, Missis. This was all my fault."

I knew the slap was coming. It stung like a flame. Then I felt her hand grasp my ear as she pulled me out of the room and back towards the servants' stairs. She practically threw me down them.

"This is no place for you! Go downstairs and you stay downstairs until I come down and tan the hide off of you!"

She closed the door to the servants' staircase. I listened hard, and prayed and prayed she would not find Mary. I rubbed my ear. It felt like she had almost pulled it off, and the skin on my cheek stung. I went back to the kitchen. Missis Palmer would be down soon. The length of the beating I would get would depend on whether she decided to tell the old mistress she'd found me upstairs.

Cook came in as I was thinking, rolling her sleeves up and putting water on to boil.

"Where is that Mary Lee when you need her?" She said it to herself as much as me.

At that second, Mary came in with a bucket of ashes in her hand.

"Here, Cook!" she said. "I'll just empty this."

She hooked her arm in mine as we walked out into the garden.

"She didn't see you?" I asked.

"No! Nat, I can't thank you enough. Will she hit you hard?"

I half smiled. "I thought I'd be free here," I said. "How could we all be so wrong?"

Up in the sky flew small birds, not bright like hummingbirds back home, but dark blue, almost black. They were shaped like scythes and swooped high in the sky. They could go anywhere they liked.

Mamma and Martha were depending on me. I had sworn I would come home. I had sworn I would free us all.

"It's not fair," Mary said, low. "That you belong to them, that they can do what they like to you. I know I get the back of Cook's hand but they can't sell me."

I looked back at the house and down at my two whole feet. Why should I stay in this house a moment longer? If I could find my way to Henry, to the inn in Shadwell, he would help, I was sure of it. I knew I had to act now. Why wait for more bruises?

"Go inside, Mary," I said. "If she asks, tell Missis Palmer you didn't see me."

Mary looked anxious. "What! Where are you going?"

"To find my friend Henry Hughes," I said. "To be free."

I walked to the garden door and out into the mews. I walked fast, over the cobbles, past the stables, then out into a busy street. I thought I heard someone shout. Missis Palmer? I did not turn back.

I broke into a run.

CHAPTER

I kept running and running for what felt like hours, down what seemed like a thousand streets, all lined with high buildings, until my feet were so sore that I had to stop. I bent over, gulping in air.

I straightened up and tried to take my bearings. The sun was setting in the west, and Shadwell, where Henry lived, was in the east, wasn't it? I hoped Henry was still there at his sister's inn, and wasn't already sailing off across the world. Henry had said the inn was by the river, but I could not see or smell water close by. I looked round again – and I shook my head. I could not believe it. The garden square looked exactly the same as the one I'd fled. A knot of children thronged in the square; some kind of music was playing, a violin perhaps. There were the same young trees with new green leaves. My heart hammered in my chest. Had I made all that effort, run 'til my feet were cracked and bleeding only to come full circle?

I grasped the railings in front of a tall white townhouse and tried to steady myself. The front door banged open. A footman in gold-braided livery and white gloves came out. He shouted at me, his voice low and threatening.

"Get off with you!"

I staggered away and back out on to the pavement and into the road. How would I get anywhere in this city if everything looked the same? What if I'd never get away from the Barratts however far I ran?

"Ho there!" a voice yelled behind me, and I turned round. Coming straight for me were two huge carriage horses, eyes rolling, hooves flying. The driver yelled again. I felt a sharp stab of fear as I thought the horses would most certainly run me down. Perhaps I wanted them to? Then there'd be no more running. The moment stretched on, and I felt the ground thunder under my poor sore feet. I shut my eyes.

A hand closed round my arm and pulled me hard. The carriage clattered by so close I swear I felt the horses' breath hot upon my cheek.

I looked up at the man who had pulled me back. He held me tight and looked as angry as the footman.

"What are you thinking?" The accent was American. The face was darker-skinned than my own.

"Sir. . ." I thought perhaps I must be in some kind of waking dream, because this man, taller than twice my height, wore a tricorn hat that carried a model ship. A full-rigged three-master, not unlike a miniature of *The Brave Venture*. He looked at me hard, and I could see he was worried not angry. He took in my feet and his face tightened. He marched me back to the square and picked up a violin.

"You should come with me," he said in a low voice. "If anyone asks, tell them I'm your father."

I tried to pull away. Could I trust him?

He bent down and his eyes were dark brown and uneasy. "I know what you are," he said. "I can help."

I was still frozen. He loosened his grip and I rubbed my arm.

"Please." He spoke gently now.

I looked up at the model boat again and suddenly I remembered what Mary Lee had said. "You are Mr Shadrack Furman! You are the dancer, aren't you?"

His face cracked into a smile, and I saw there was warmth there. "Indeed I am, young man. Born on the Guinea coast and broken in Charlotte, Carolina, across the Atlantic, in America. I have a trade that is not dancing, but as an old soldier of the Royal Ethiopian regiment I am forebade work. But see –" he began to open his jacket and pulled his shirt away from his collarbone: there was a mark, a brand, of interlocking letters – "if I am not mistaken we have much in common." He saw me nod and covered up again.

He put out his hand and I took it. Freely this time.

"Are you enslaved?" I asked, quietly, in case someone heard.

"Not any more." We started walking.

"I need to get to Shadwell," I said. Mr Furman led me across a busy road and down a street of shops and businesses. I went on. "I have a friend there, in an inn called The Cat and Mutton. . ."

"You shouldn't be out on the street on your own," he said. "I doubt if I'm wrong, but I reckon as folk will be looking for you soon enough."

I remembered the notices Mary Lee had read out loud: money offered for escaped slaves. I followed him down the street of shops.

"Let's get you off the road for tonight," he said, looking round as if he might see a crowd of people already after me. "This might be a happy accident, for I am on my way to a meeting with my brothers, the Sons of Africa. We're going to make sure there ain't never any more slaves, one way or another." He smiled, and even though my feet were sore and I was hungry, I couldn't help smiling back.

I would have asked there and then who the Sons of Africa were but I had never seen anything like the shops we passed: bowed-glass windows, bright coloured fronts, red and blue and yellow. Gloves displayed in fans like flowers, hats, lace, china that the old mistress would love in her house and that the young master would love to smash.

But I didn't have time to stare as Mr Furman went along at a clip. We turned off into a street of bakers and saddlers, shops of the more useful sort, and he pulled me into a grocer's shop. Inside, it was warm and smelled of coffee and spices and my stomach groaned with hunger. I had not eaten a thing since some bread and butter at breakfast.

Mr Furman removed his hat. There was a tall brown woman at the counter with bright skin and black braided hair, she was such a beauty I was struck dumb for a moment. But as soon as she saw me she frowned.

"Another one!" she said, folding her arms. "Mr Furman, what if his owners find out? What if they call the magistrates?"

"Frances, please. What's the use in fighting for an end to slavery if we can't help our own children. . ."

The young woman sighed, pushed her braids away from her face.

"You're right, of course." She looked me up and down. "Let me find him a warmer coat, I have many younger brothers, we should have something to fit."

"A pair of boots for my friend would be welcome, Frances," Mr Furman said.

"Boots do not grow on trees, Mr Furman."

"Shadrack, please."

It seemed as if they were talking about a parcel. "I am here – and I am grateful – but I don't want to cause any trouble for you." I nodded at her. And at Mr Furman, "Sir."

"A polite lad, then." She smiled at me and put out her hand. "I am Miss Frances Sancho, this shop was my father's. He too suffered enslavement. And you are?"

"Nathaniel Barratt, late of Barratt Hall, Jamaica." I wiped my hand before I shook hers. "If someone could put me on the road to Shadwell then I would not need to trouble you. . ."

Frances shook her head. "Forgive me, you are no trouble at all, Master Nathaniel. The world outside is dangerous, and it will soon be dark."

Mr Furman led the way upstairs to the rooms above the shop and into a parlour. There were a few well stuffed chairs set around a fireplace. It was not half as grand as any of the Barratts' houses, but it was clean and bright.

"Are the others coming?" Mr Furman said. "Equiano? Cugoano?"

"All of them," Frances said.

"And Granville Sharp?"

"Mr Sharp will definitely be here. Said he's bringing the witness, the first mate." Miss Sancho lifted the lid of a linen chest and took out a dark woollen jacket and unfolded it. She held it up against me. "This one ought to do."

Mr Furman looked out of the window to the street as if expecting the company to arrive this instant. My stomach rumbled louder than the traffic below.

Miss Sancho smiled at me. "Let me fetch you some broth."

I put on the jacket, made of good thick material, and with pockets. When Miss Sancho returned with a large bowl of broth I fair wolfed it down. It was hot and with plenty of mutton, I swear I'd not tasted anything as good my whole life.

Mr Furman and Miss Sancho continued talking as she set out wood and kindling in the fireplace and lit the candles in the room. I scraped every last drop of that broth from the bowl and felt warm both inside and out for the first time since I had set foot in this country. I moved myself closer to a small armchair by the fireside and pulled the jacket around me. Slowly, in the flicker of candlelight, I felt my eyes fall shut.

CHAPTER

I woke with a start. It was dark outside now but the fire burned orange in the grate. There were footsteps on the stairs, men talking loudly. I sat up. I could not help feeling afraid. Was I really safe here with these people? I heard Mr Furman's voice, and relaxed a little. I stepped softly to the door to listen. Four or five men, maybe six, all talking across each other. On their way downstairs, by the sound of it. There was mention of the *Zong* and I racked my brains to remember when I had last heard that name. By the time I opened the door a crack, the men had gone downstairs.

I crept to the head of the stairs and listened to the group of men gathered in the hall. Mr Furman was talking to a soberly dressed white man with a small powdered wig. He clapped him on the back. "Mr Sharp –" he turned to another man that I couldn't see from where I was perched on the stairs – "Mr Equiano. I have no doubt that with the help of Mr Kelsall here we will turn the tide. We will make the British see what the cost of slavery is, and that we are human, not cargo."

"What I saw was a most horrid brutality, sirs. . ." said another voice. I could not see the man who spoke, but my ears pricked. Didn't I know him? And that name – Mr Kelsall. Could that really be the mate? The same man from *The Brave Venture*? I heard the street door open. The men were leaving, Mr Furman was saying his farewells.

I went to follow but Frances Sancho came out across the landing with a candle and called to me.

"Nathaniel?"

"I have to go, madam!" I started down the stairs.

I ran down just as Mr Furman was bolting the front door shut.

"Nathaniel! Whoa there, young fellow." He blocked the door. "You're not going anywhere on your own."

"But I need to know – that Mr Kelsall? Is he a sailor?"

Mr Furman looked at me. Frances set down her candle. They seemed so calm, but all I could think was that my only link to Henry Hughes was walking further away with every moment.

"I think he can help me! My friend Henry Hughes, Kelsall knows him, he could take me back to Shadwell, to the inn. . ."

I was talking too fast, I knew.

"Take a breath, young man." Mr Furman put a hand on my shoulder and steered me towards a high stool by the shop counter. "How do you know Kelsall?"

Frances set the candle down. They both studied me.

"You weren't a survivor on the *Zong*? Another witness? Did you see all those people thrown overboard?" Frances spoke softly, but I could see the shock on her face.

I shook my head. She nodded; I think she was relieved on my account.

"Mr Kelsall needs his rest, and so do you." Mr Furman leaned upon the shop counter.

"If Mr Kelsall could tell Henry where I am…"

"Henry? Your friend the sailor?"

"Yes, I met them both on the boat over from Jamaica. And that's where I was going when you found me on the street – to see Henry Hughes at The Cat and Mutton in Shadwell!" I said.

Mr Furman laughed. "As I remember you seemed to be going to heaven or hell under the hooves of some rather large horses."

Then I told them about Mamma and Martha, about the old mistress and young master and being sold to a duke from somewhere called Mistleton in Yorkshire. That I needed to find Henry as soon as I could, before he found himself another place on another boat. He could help me find work, and that's what I needed to do – earn money. When I had finished my story, the candle had burned half the way down. Frances fetched us all some small beer and Mr Furman sighed.

"Henry must wait," Mr Furman said. "Tomorrow is important for us Sons of Africa."

"Are they all your brothers?" I asked.

Mr Furman shook his head. "Brothers in name only. We're a like-minded group, some African by birth, others from across the world like me, or born and bred in Britain, all with one aim: to find an end to slavery."

Frances put three mugs of beer down on the counter. "My father was among them," she said, glowing with pride. "Ignatius Sancho, the first black man to vote in the general election!"

She rolled up her sleeves and took a cloth from under the counter to mop up the spills and then she gave Mr Furman a sharp look. "I don't see why you won't have Daughters of Africa at your blessed meetings..."

Mr Furman winked at me and drank his beer.

"You have both been very kind," I said. "If I can talk to Mr Kelsall I'm sure he will know the way to Shadwell."

"Tomorrow is the trial. Mr Kelsall will be busy – maybe afterwards."

Frances pulled a stool out for me from behind the counter. "Did you hear what happened with the *Zong*, then, Nathaniel?" she asked.

I was quiet. I thought of what Mr Kelsall had said to me and Henry about the sharks, about the people dying and the sea turning red. I looked at Frances and then Mr Furman. "How many died?" I asked. "How many were thrown overboard?"

"One hundred and thirty two. Children in their mothers' arms."

I shivered thinking of Martha and Mamma.

Mr Furman shook his head. "And men too. Your Mr Kelsall was on that boat and tried to stop them, but he was overruled."

No wonder poor Mr Kelsall was so melancholy, I thought.

"This trial is vital," he continued. "Maybe the most important there's been. If we can get the papers to print every word of what happened, and ordinary folk read about it, then maybe this could be the beginning of the end of this awful trade."

"I don't understand. . ." I said. "Who is on trial? Mr Kelsall? For killing all those people?"

"No, son, the owners of the boat."

"For throwing all those people overboard?"

Mr Furman shook his head. "Not even that. The owners of the *Zong* are arguing with their insurance company. They claim they had no choice but to massacre all those children, all those men and women. They went to court to claim money from their insurers for the death of all those people."

I frowned. "I don't understand, Mr Furman. This isn't a crime?"

Frances tried to explain. The captain and the ship owners, she said, had paid for something called insurance. The trial tomorrow was a dispute between the ship owners and the insurance company. It was all about money.

Mr Furman sipped his beer. "These devils. They are clever. They make money whether we live or die."

I still didn't understand. "What is insurance, miss?" I asked. Frances paused, looking thoughtful.

"Nothing more than a kind of bet, or wager against disaster or loss," said Mr Furman. He must have seen my confusion because he smiled, then put his ship hat down on the shop counter.

"See this ship? Say it's carrying. . ." He looked around and picked up some tea leaves from a small brown sack. "It's carrying this tea." He tipped a handful of leaves on to the deck of the model ship. "All the way from across the sea and back home to London. They spent a lot of money on that tea and plan to sell it just as soon as they get home." He steered his ship hat across the counter. "But if something happens. . ."

"A storm!" Frances pulled her braids back from her face and blew hard across the ship, scattering tea leaves everywhere.

Mr Furman nodded. "Then the ship owners will have no money from the sale of the tea. They will be out of pocket. They might be ruined,"

"But with insurance," Frances said, "the owners will have paid a small amount to an insurance company in advance, just in case something of that nature happened, and when they come back to London and say they lost their cargo, the insurers pay up. Cover their costs."

"The ship owners won't make the fortune they'd have got from selling that tea, but they get enough to pay everyone, to keep things sweet." Mr Furman brushed the last of the tea leaves off his hat.

"But the *Zong*?" I said. "That wasn't tea."

"Exactly." Mr Furman pulled his ship hat back towards our side of the counter.

"The Captain of the *Zong* packed his ship – built for taking two hundred men, women and children – with over four hundred souls."

Frances wiped down the counter. "They were packed and chained below decks, with no room to sit." She sounded grim.

I nodded. I had heard the tales of the Middle Passage, the trip from Africa across the Caribbean. It was hell on earth.

"Folk were lying deep in their own filth." Frances spat the words. "It was no wonder people sickened."

"And died," Mr Furman went on. "Forty and then sixty, then the fever spread to the crew. Captain Collingwood was a lousy sailor – he'd taken the voyage to make his fortune. He worried he'd not make the money he wanted with ill slaves."

My eyes widened. "So he threw folk overboard for the insurance money?"

"Exactly so, young man. Exactly so. One hundred and thirty two men, women and children. . ."

"But he is not on trial for murder?"

Frances laughed, a bitter laugh. Mr Furman sailed his ship hat back towards us.

"Captain Collingwood died three days after they made land. God's justice, I reckon. He said there was not enough water on board for everyone, and that he'd had no choice but to kill those people to save the crew. But Kelsall says that's a lie." Shadrack Furman leaned on the bar counter. "The trial is all about money. See, the insurers wouldn't pay out. And the ship owners want their money."

"So why is this trial important, if no one will be brought to justice?" I asked.

"This is a way to change minds, Nathaniel!" Frances said. "If enough ordinary English people read about this case, hear what terrible things are done to our brothers and sisters for money, that can only be a good thing!"

CHAPTER

I thought I would be staying with Frances Sancho but Mr Furman took me back to his lodgings through the dark London streets. He reminded me to tell anyone who asked that I was his son.

In the streets, torches flared against the darkness. There was so much to see: pie sellers and street musicians, a girl with a dancing dog. There was a lightness to my step, even though I wore new (to me) boots that rubbed my toes. Was this what freedom felt like? Everything seemed interesting, everything sharper. Even the bad smells.

As we crossed the road, Mr Furman waved at a man driving a wagon. As it came closer, the smell was so strong I thought I would be sick. Mr Furman talked to the driver but I stayed back. The smell was the worst I'd ever known, worse than the stink of rotten food, or horse manure.

Mr Furman said his farewells and laughed at me. "That's the night-soil man. Only have them in the cities, I expect you've never seen the like."

"Night soil?" I asked. "What's that?"

"Soil as in dirt. Human dirt. They empty the closets in the houses. Dig the stuff out of the cesspits. And those men take it out of the city."

"A cart full of—"

Mr Furman cut in. "You got it, Nathaniel. Those fellows only work in the dark when the ladies and gentlemen are asleep. My friend Colley makes a good living out of what he gets for free."

"How does he do that?"

"Sells it. There's farmers pay him well."

"Like horse manure?" I asked.

"Exactly that! I tell you, Nathaniel, I couldn't do it, but Colley, he doesn't smell a thing any more."

I asked how he knew the man and Mr Furman told me that he had fought alongside Colley on the British side in the American War of Independence. He explained how the British had promised the slaves in America their freedom if they fought the rebels who wanted America to be a new country, and not part of Great Britain. And how his own wife and child were sold into the south before he could find them.

"I have a daughter not much younger than you in America, in Maryland," he said. "If she is still alive." He looked away and wiped a tear. I did not want to ask if he would see them again.

"Why do they do it, Mr Furman?" I asked. "Why do they treat us this way? Hurt us, sell us, send our families away."

Mr Furman thought for a long time. "Because they can." He looked up at the sky. "But one thing I always held on to, all those years I was enslaved; they might have your body, but they can never have your mind. Be free inside."

I nodded. But I had decided, I would never let anyone buy or sell me ever again.

Mr Furman promised that tomorrow, after the trial, he'd find someone to take me out of the city. I wanted to ask again about The Cat and Mutton, but thought I would keep that question for Mr Kelsall when I spoke to him after the trial. He'd know where Henry was.

We walked the rest of the way in silence. Mr Furman's room was up four sets of stairs. I thought we would almost reach the moon there were so many. The house was full of noise too. Outside in the street, a pig snuffled through rubbish, inside dogs barked, babies cried and an argument raged on a floor below. But even so, this was the room of a free man and it felt to me like the best place in the whole world.

I would have been happy to sleep in the armchair, which was losing its stuffing but looked comfortable enough. Mr Furman, however, insisted that I take the bed. And as soon as I hit the mattress I slept, dreaming of sunlight and a world without the old mistress, her son, or her parrot. My first night as a free man.

When I woke, Mr Furman had made a small fire to heat some water for tea.

"It will be a long day, Mr Barratt," he said.

"I have never been to a trial," I said. "Once one of the field hands, Naomi she was called, was said to have stolen some callaloo – that's like spinach – from another woman's vegetable patch. But Naomi swore blind that callaloo was her own! Old Thomas – he was the gardener and one of the oldest slaves on the plantation – was set to deciding which woman was telling the truth. He made them share." I shook my head. "I couldn't have done it. How can you tell who is telling the truth when folk lie so easily?"

Mr Furman nodded. "Folk open their mouth and lies fall out. But this is different, this trial. Oh, it's not simply about whether some rich white folk get richer, this is about whether we are human beings or blocks of wood."

He sighed. I didn't say anything. Truth was, I couldn't imagine those folk that owned slaves, that forced us to work for nothing, wanted to see us as more than something they could buy or sell – or throw overboard.

After a mug of tea, we walked to Westminster. I had never seen such buildings! The Abbey was bigger than anything I could have imagined, with its pointy spires and towers. I could not believe mere men had built it. Mr Furman laughed and said I should see St Paul's Cathedral. Then we reached Westminster Hall, an old square building black with dirt, and Mr Furman told me that once the English had tried their own king here, a long time ago. And cut his head off! I thought if they could do that to their own king, then perhaps anything was possible.

And there were so many people! Mr Furman said all the black and brown folk of London would be here to see what happened, and it looked like he was right. Footmen and chairmen in their masters' fine livery. Women in colourful silk and satins, with hats that must have cost the same as a maid's annual earnings. Working men and women in aprons and boots. Folk off the street in no boots at all. Then I saw one man, white and heavy-built, head and shoulders above most of the crowd, big as a mountain. I thought I was imagining it at first but he was staring right at me. I felt a flicker of fear and pulled my cap down over my eyes, drawing close to Mr Furman.

We followed the crowd and went inside, past stalls selling oranges and nuts, and up some wooden stairs to a kind of gallery above the open space of the court. Mr Furman seemed to know everyone, and I thought it would take all day to find our seats as he stopped to talk to so many folk. I recognized some of the fellows from last night, sober-suited men with grey hair. Mr Furman pulled me over.

"Nathaniel! Meet Mr Equiano. His name, mark my words, will be known across the world in time."

Equiano shook his head and took my hand.

Mr Furman went on. "He is writing his life story, Nat."

Mr Equiano smiled. "I doubt a soul will read it."

"Capture and freedom? What better story is there, man?" Mr Furman said and I thought I agreed.

I was astonished – a black man, writing his own story! I thought books were for white people. Maybe it would be worth learning my letters if only to be able to read Mr Equiano's book. Or perhaps, one day, to have the chance to tell my own story, to write it up and have folk read it.

"He bought and paid for his own freedom," Mr Furman said. I would have liked to have asked how much it had cost, but Mr Furman was already introducing me to another man.

"And this here is Mr Granville Sharp."

He was a white man, sharp by name and by features, I thought.

"Good morning, Mr Sharp," I said. The gentleman took my hand and shook it, ordinary as anything. His smile was warm. I looked for Mr Kelsall but there was no sign. I crossed my fingers behind my back. He had to be here! I tried to listen to the gentleman's conversation but the general noise of the crowd made it hard. Mr Sharp had written to all the newspapers, he said.

"This is an offence against God. We have the Lord Mansfield making the judgement, the foremost legal mind in all of England."

"Aye," answered Equiano, "and the slave owners have the Solicitor General to argue for their side."

"We should be able to speak for ourselves!" Mr Furman said and I have to say I agreed with him.

Mr Equiano put an arm on Mr Furman's shoulder. "We have to follow the rules."

"Their rules, man. . ."

Mr Equiano sighed. "One day, Shadrack, one day we will all be as free as they are."

"I hope to heaven I live long enough to see that. . ."

Granville Sharp nodded. "As long as we English exploit our fellow men then none of us is free."

I looked at Mr Sharp. I thought he had a clever face.

"And Mr Kelsall?" Mr Furman asked. Mr Equiano looked down into the court below. I looked too and saw the first mate of *The Brave Venture* waiting to play his part. I almost waved but thought he would not see me up here. Mr Kelsall seemed nervous, tugging at his collar, eyes darting around the court.

Suddenly a call came from the court "All Rise!" The crowd stood up. A white man came in, wearing a bright red robe – I thought it was a dress at first – and a long powdered wig. I spotted Frances Sancho waving us over. The man in the robe and wig sat down. Mr Equiano, Mr Sharp, Mr Furman and I all settled down on the bench next to Frances.

"That's Lord Mansfield himself," she whispered,

and passed round a bag full of oranges. I took one and slipped it into my pocket for later.

Even though we were high up I could hear almost every word that was said in court. It seemed to carry up into the roof clear as a bell. The crowd around us in the gallery gasped as the details of the case were set out by yet another man in a wig, although his was not so long as Lord Mansfield's. He spoke with his chest puffed out, and his voice was silky. Mr Furman whispered that he was the Solicitor General, the man arguing that the ship's crew did the right thing in throwing all those people overboard.

He said how the Zong carried far too many slaves for its size, but that Captain Collingwood had only ever tried to save as much of his cargo as he could. He threw some of the cargo overboard because there had not been enough water for everyone.

"Cargo!" Mr Furman cursed under his breath.

The Solicitor General went on. "On November the twenty-ninth, fifty-four slaves, women and children, were thrown overboard, and then, on December the first forty-two men. Over the following few days another thirty-six men were thrown into the sea alive. It was not an attempt to claim insurance," the Solicitor General looked around the court. Watching in the gallery, the crowd hissed until we were told to quiet.

"Remember, gentlemen, this is not a murder trial!" the Solicitor General said. "This is merely about property, about the disposal of goods and the proper payment of insurance."

The Solicitor General went on. "These slaves, they were all property, not humans. We are not talking about matters of cruelty!"

I would have thrown something at him if I could. But down on the floor of the court the men seemed to think there was nothing at all wrong with what he had said.

"How can he say that?" Frances Sancho said. Mr Furman looked just as furious.

Then Lord Mansfield, our man, got up and reminded the court that the captain's log – his diary – was missing.

"When the ship docked at Black River, Jamaica, it was found that over four hundred gallons of fresh drinking water were on board. Enough for every member of the crew and cargo," he said. I wanted to cheer. Here at last was someone fighting for us. But then he went on. "Whether this is a case of right or wrong is not at stake here."

I could not believe it! How could anybody think that this wasn't about right and wrong! Everyone in the gallery sat up, stiff and silent.

"This is merely a case of goods and chattels, as the Solicitor General says," said Lord Mansfield. "This is merely to discover whether the insurance company should pay out to the *Zong*'s owners."

I looked at Frances. Her eyes blazed and I saw Mr Furman squeeze her hand to try and calm her even though I thought he was fit to explode with fury too, as his teeth were set hard. Mr Equiano sighed. I heard him try to explain: "This is a long game we are playing here." But I had stopped listening.

One grey wig droned on after another, and another. Mr Kelsall said his piece, his voice was just as sad as I remembered. He took off his hat and ran the brim through his hands. I hoped the judge would feel as sorry for him as I did. He did not speak well and the Solicitor General made him out to be a fool who had been dismissed by the captain and so sought to make out that Collingwood was in the wrong.

Then Lord Mansfield summed up. Mr Furman took Frances's hand and the whole gallery strained to listen. I barely heard the verdict. I was concentrating so hard on watching Mr Kelsall, to keep an eye on where he went. But when the cheer went up from the gallery, I knew that Lord Mansfield had made the decision against the ship owners. No insurance would be paid. But there was to be no punishment either. I didn't see why this was such a great cause for celebration, but Mr Sharp was thrilled.

"The way is open now! I will bring a murder case against those ship owners, you wait and see!" he said, clapping Equiano on the back. "There will be justice."

"And I hope I see the day," Mr Equiano said, "when black men and women will no longer be property!"

Then the men started talking about liberty and freedom. Mr Furman and Miss Sancho were conversing, heads close together. I thought of Henry and my own liberty – I had to get out of the city.

Quietly, I made my way down the wooden stairs to find Mr Kelsall. Down in the court, it was a crush.

Men and women streamed out of the hall. I was swept up in the crowd, struggling against the tide of people as I was pushed into the square to Westminster Bridge. Finally, I managed to weave out of the chaos, and caught my breath. By the time I had got back to the hall, the crowd had thinned. I saw Lord Mansfield, without his red robe, step into a waiting Sedan Chair, and the two chairmen carry him off.

By the door of the court a boy my own age, but lighter skinned, was singing a song about never working again. He wore a suit of clothes made of silver brocade, slightly less showy than the one Missis Palmer would have made me wear. He also had a silver collar around his neck, like that of a dog only bigger. I tried not to stare.

He stopped. "You on the lam?"

I shrugged. I had no idea what he meant.

The boy went on. "I am Mr Percy's pageboy at Hanover Square, well the Mistress Percy's, in all fact."

I did not know what to say. Was he proud of his enslavement? I ignored him and looked around for Mr Kelsall. I was beginning to worry I might have missed him already. Then a note of fear crept into my thoughts. What if I couldn't even find Mr Furman? Or the Sanchos? What if I was lost again?

"The Percys aren't so bad," the silver-suited boy went on. "I wait at tables and walk in front of my lady's chair."

I was still looking around and he tugged at my sleeve. "Hey! Who owns you, or are you free as the air?"

"Me? Mr Barratt, only I do not know the address," I said without thinking. I looked at him and swallowed. I should have kept my mouth shut. Could I trust him just because we shared the same skin colour?

"Are you lost then? If you need anything, just ask. I am always ready –" he bowed a little – "to help a brother."

I hesitated. He smiled a friendly smile.

"Do you know Shadwell?" I began, but then relief flooded me because I spotted the face I was looking for, standing in the street a few metres away.

"Mr Kelsall!" I shouted out. I mumbled an 'excuse me' to the silver boy and ran towards Mr Kelsall waving. I shouted again. "Mr Kelsall! It's me, Nathaniel. Nathaniel Barratt!"

The man turned, he met my eye, and as he did so someone grabbed me from behind. It was the man I'd seen inside the hall, the massive mountain-sized man who'd been staring at me. He gathered me up as easily as if I were a piece of cloth. My arms were pinned to my sides and the force of the grip was so strong that I thought my bones would snap in two.

"Let go, sir!" My legs were off the ground. The man threw me into the back of a wagon and before I could jump out, he tied my hands behind my back.

"That's the one." The boy in the silver suit nodded. "He belongs to the Barratts, Mr Gemson, like you thought. He told me himself."

The silver-clothed boy put out his hand. "I'll take my finder's fee now, thank you."

The man mountain dropped some coins into his hand. The boy turned and walked away before I could curse him. I looked around wildly for Mr Furman or anyone I knew, but the wagon jolted forward and I fell face down into the bottom of the cart. I was free no longer.

CHAPTER

The cart rolled to a stop outside the Barratts' house. Mr Gemson rang the bell and one of the footmen thanked him as he heaved me out of the cart and set me down on the pavement. The footman told Mr Gemson to wait for his reward.

"You're in for it now!" the footman said to me, his hand gripping my shoulder hard.

Suddenly there was a sharp shout. "You're to bring him with me. Master Barratt will see him in the library!"

Missis Palmer stood on the front steps. Her expression was closed up and stony, like always. The footman marched me over, and as soon as I came close she slapped me hard around the face.

"You ungrateful wretch, Nathaniel Barratt!"

My face stung like it was on fire. I heard the door in the front area open and saw Mary had come out of the kitchen. She was standing in the lower doorway watching. She looked furious. I shook my head. There was nothing she could do.

The footman held my arm with a grip of iron and fair hauled me up the grand staircase behind Missis Palmer. I tried to tell myself to keep my chin up, but my knees felt weak. Missis Palmer opened the door to the library – it was the room she had found me in with Mary. I thought that was not a good omen.

I looked around. It was quiet, apart from the clock ticking and the fire crackling, and first of all I thought the room was empty. But as Missis Palmer shut the door behind her, I saw the young master at the window holding a glass of wine. He was smiling, but I knew he would not be sympathetic. It was a very unpleasant smile.

"Nathaniel, isn't it?" he said and took a drink. "You have been a great disappointment." My shoulders ached from having my hands tied together behind my back and I longed to shake them free. But I kept as still as possible, while he watched me like a cat eyeing up its next meal. He drained his wine glass. "Have you nothing to say?" He crossed the room and stood in front of me. I could smell his breath: wine and tobacco.

I opened my mouth to say sorry, but before I realized what was happening he threw me on to the floor and kicked me. I saw his shiny boot coming towards me and the pain shot through my body. I could not shield my face with my hands so I curled into a ball as the blows rained down. Then the door opened. I turned my head to see the old mistress with Mr Bird sitting on her shoulder. Missis Palmer stood behind her. The young master's boot stopped, mid swing. The old mistress curled her lip and stood over me.

"Get up, ungrateful child. Or I might tell Mr Bird to take your eye out. After all, where you're going one eye is just as good as two."

It was hard to get up with my hands still tied. I knew Mr Bird's beak would rip my eyelids open and pluck out my eyeball easy as slicing a grape.

"There's a ship at the start of next week. We are sending you back," the old mistress said. "You are old enough for the field – and certainly not suitable as a gift for a duke and duchess."

Even though my ribs still hurt from the kicking I could not help a small smile. I would be closer to Mamma and Martha. And even though they would have me break my back in the field I would see Thomas again...

"The idiot smiles," the young master said, and I remembered to make my face blank again. "He will not smile with half a foot and only one eye."

I swallowed again. How would I make it over the mountains to the free towns of the Maroons with half a foot? What about Martha? How would Mamma carry her with me to help too? My eyes were prickling. I blinked.

The old mistress smiled, and I bit back the tears. They would not make me cry. She and Missis Palmer swished away and the young master poured himself another glass of wine. I swallowed, my heart sinking. He hadn't finished with me. I stood as tall as I could given my bruising.

"Ungrateful devil," the young master said. He drew back his hand and knocked me to the ground. My head hit the floor with a loud smack and the world went dark.

I remembered nothing until I woke up the next morning. My ribs hurt something rotten. But at least I still had my two eyes and feet. I could hear the church bells ringing and thought it must be Sunday. I could see I was in an attic room, with a low sloping roof. I was lying on the floor with my face against the bare boards. Every part of my body ached. How long had I been here? I wondered what Mr Furman was doing. Was he worrying about me, or had he forgotten me already? Would he be out in the square this afternoon, dancing, like Mary said, the ship on his hat rolling over pretend seas? I should have asked him to show me when I had the chance. I could be free in my head, couldn't I? What did Mamma say? *Walk tall, they cannot hurt us.*

They have hurt us so hard and for so long. What more can one blow do?

I blinked away the tears and rubbed my eyes. Outside the church bells kept on ringing. My mouth was dry and my lips were cracked. I reached up to touch them and felt a tiny flash of joy as I realized someone had untied my hands. I stretched my arms out, hearing the bones in my shoulders pop, and looked around. The room was full of old furniture, boxes and paintings propped up against each other. A small window was set into the roof and on the sill – my heart leaped again – was a bowl of water and some grapes. I sat up, even though it hurt to do so. I would gulp that water down then plan my escape. By the look of it the window was unlocked, perhaps my luck had changed.

But then a horrible screech cut through the air. There was a flapping of wings, and Mr Bird flew down from the pile of broken furniture. He settled on the windowsill, and I realized with dismay that the water was his, the bowl splattered with his mess. Mr Bird skittered sideways on its horrible claws and claimed the grapes too. It pulled the bunch apart with its scaly claws and stabbed the point of its beak hard into the grape. All the while looking straight at me with its shiny black-button eyes.

"Horrid boy! Horrid boy!" It laughed and stretched out its wings. No wonder they'd untied me. That creature would watch me better than any guard dog. The minute I opened that window, or tried to escape, Mr Bird would raise the alarm.

I sat down against the wall. My mouth was drier than a bowl of ashes. On the windowsill the grapes looked fat and juicy, but I knew better than to try and take anything of Mr Bird's. I had, after all, lost a finger when I was small and hungry. I had reached out for a piece of banana the parrot had dropped. Quick as a flash it had pecked it off. Snapped right through the bone with that heavy black beak. Even then I knew better than to cry out and risk a blow from the old mistress, so I just ran back to our hut and cried and cried. That bird was the devil with feathers.

I shut my eyes, defeated. If only I had waited with Mr Furman, if only I had not told that boy my name! Now I'd never be able to earn any money and buy Mamma's or Martha's freedom. I wouldn't even be able to buy my own the way Mr Equiano had done.

Nor fight in a war to earn it neither, like Mr Furman or his night-soil friend. I turned my face away from the window and cursed my own foolishness.

Then I felt something in my pocket. It was the orange Frances had given me at the trial. It was a little battered and bruised but I took it out of my pocket and peeled it with my fingers. Tasting it felt like a celebration. I was wasting time and energy feeling sorry for myself. I allowed myself just half of the squashed segments – I might need the others later – and thought about how I could get out. I would not give up yet.

The door was locked, although whether it was a key or a bolt on the outside I could not tell. Either way, getting down the house by the servants' staircase would be impossible without being discovered. Somehow I would have to get past that bird.

A sudden knock at the door made me jump out of my skin.

"Nathaniel? Nat!" It was Mary Lee.

Mr Bird squawked and I tried to shush him. When that didn't work I threw him a precious segment of my orange.

"Listen!" Mary sounded excited. "I saw Mr Furman

on the way back from church. I made sure to tell him you were here. You are not forgotten!"

"They have the parrot guarding me." I leaned against the door. "If I open the window or try to climb down, he will raise the alarm."

"Won't he just fly away?" Mary asked.

I sighed. "Mr Bird came out of his egg the day the old mistress was born." I lowered my voice. "Sometimes I think she can see what that parrot sees, hear what it hears. . ." I looked at it. It was still watching me.

"You must not give up hope! Mr Furman has found Henry and between us all we will make a plan." I heard her get up quickly.

"Tell me!" I felt a rush of relief. They had found Henry! I was not forgotten.

"I have to go. I will be back but I have to work. The party for the duke and duchess is this evening and Cook is making all kinds of dainties."

"The plan?" I cut in. "Is there a key for the door?"

"Missis Palmer has it, and anyway the house is full of people!"

"What do you think I should do then?" I said impatiently. "Climb out of the window?"

"Yes! That's it! The window!" I heard Mary start to go downstairs.

"What about Mr Bird?" I said, but I was talking to myself. I slumped against the door and watched the parrot demolish the orange segment. I imagined he could go to work just like that on my eyeballs if I got too close.

How could I get past him? Trouble was I couldn't even look out of the window with that parrot in the way. And even if I did, I knew I was four floors up. If there was any justice, I thought, that creature would drop down dead.

Perhaps if I could climb down as far as the garden wall… No, it would still be too high to jump safely to the ground. I would break my arm or leg, wouldn't I?

Outside I could hear comings and goings in the garden as the servants prepared for the party, but I dared not get close enough to the window to look.

Mr Bird sat himself down in a patch of sunshine and ruffled his feathers, cleaned them through with his beak and turned round. Was he going to sleep? But the parrot only shook itself. "Horrid boy! Horrid boy!" he said, his head bobbing up and down.

"Mr Bird, shush now." I tried talking to it as if it were a particularly ugly baby. My tone of voice did not seem to work. It only shouted louder.

"Bones and blood! Horrid boy!"

Back home, in Barratt Hall, Betsy would throw a cover – it was an old curtain – over his cage. She said the nasty-minded bird thought the darkness meant night had come, and would stop his noise. What if I waited until it fell asleep, and threw my jacket over it? Then I could wrap the parrot tight, and kept its beak closed up. So I took off my jacket and sat down as near as I dared. But time passed and it was me that dozed.

I woke with a jolt. I had dreamed I was on the top yardarm of *The Brave Venture*. Henry was telling me not to look down, but then I was falling, like a stone towards the deck.

I was desperately thirsty. I was so far gone that I was thinking of trying to sip at Mr Bird's water, but he was staring at me with his beady eyes, as far from sleep as ever. There was so much noise in the house and outside in the garden that I did not hear anyone coming up the stairs, so when Mary knocked on the door again I jumped. So did Mr Bird, of course, flapping and squawking. I fished in my pocket for the rest of the orange but I had squashed it in my sleep.

"Shhhh! Shhh!" I said, willing the bird to quiet. I tried singing the tune that Thomas used to sing sometimes; "Long time, I no see Li-za," I sang. "Water come a me eye..."

"Are you singing?" Mary whispered through the door. "I cannot stay, I have so many pots and pans to wash and scour my hands will be rubbed raw. But Mr Furman will be in the mews with a wagon at nine o'clock!"

"The mews?" I said. "But how..."

"He says you will find a way. And I say you will too. Here –" she pushed something under the door; a knife she must have taken from the kitchen – "I think those windows might be hard to open," she said. "Don't be late!" Then she was gone again, and all I could hear were the sounds of activity down in the garden, and a band striking up some dance tunes. I thought it sounded quite beautiful. I wondered who the Duke and Duchess of Mistleton's daughter was, and what she was like. Poor girl, having to spend her life in a kind of feather-bedded slavery married to the young master, hundreds of miles away from home.

Outside the church clock struck for six o'clock. I had three hours to find my way out of this room. I picked up the knife and turned it over in my hand. I had people that cared about me, not just Mamma and Martha and Thomas, but friends here. Mary and Mr Furman, and Henry too. And what could the Barratts do to me if I tried to run? Take my eye? Kill me? What was better? A short death, or a long one in a cane field under the shadow of the whip?

I looked at Mr Bird, I was still holding the knife. It was a shame, I thought, that it wasn't sharper. We stared hard at each other. I forced myself not to look away. Mr Bird opened its horrible beak and I saw its tongue, like a dried-up blackened worm. I still did not look away. I would find a way to get to open that window, even if I had to lose another finger.

It blinked.

I smiled.

"Mr Bird," I said aloud. "You will not win."

CHAPTER

10

I spent the next couple of hours searching through the furniture again. But after what seemed like ages all I had found was a couple of old paintings of sad men and sadder women, and a pair of broken chairs. Nothing, I thought, of any use... But then, finally, inside an old drawer, a canvas dustsheet. I was so happy I almost danced across the attic. The dustsheet was big and heavy enough to wrap up Mr Bird and stop his beak or claws getting anywhere near me. I imagined wrapping the parrot tight and sticking him with the knife. I would have to be quick, wouldn't he scream all the louder half-dead? The knife was small and not so sharp. Would it work? Could I do it? Kill a living thing. I had no choice. It was going to be all or nothing.

Time seemed to slow. The bell chimed for eight, and as the sky darkened the parrot quietened. I watched him ruffle his feathers and turn around, as if looking for a comfortable spot to roost. But when I shot my hand out to take one of his grapes, he squawked louder and louder, snapping his beak at me until I backed away. I stayed still, held my breath, waiting for the sound of someone on the stairs coming up to see what the bother was. But after some minutes there was nothing.

I tried the door one last time, sliding the knife in the gap and trying to trick the lock. But it would not move. The window was my only way out. I paced the room, trying to think. . . I would have to be out of that window before the hour was up. What if I was late? What if Mr Furman left in the wagon before I could find a way down?

Mr Bird was quiet again. Outside I could hear

the music and the party. A woman's laugh made the parrot look up and cock his head. I waited for Mr Bird to settle again and put the knife in my right hand, ready. Then when his head finally fell down upon his chest I held the canvas up in both my hands and shook it out, very quietly. Slowly, slowly, I tiptoed closer to the window. A floorboard creaked. I froze, still as stone. Mr Bird did not move. My heart was hammering in my chest. I crept nearer, nearer, then took my chance. I threw the sheet on top of him, used my weight to hold it tight. I felt the bird jolt awake, struggle to open its wings, felt its hard beak try and tear through the canvas. Its leathery claws scrabbled to get free. I took the knife. I was about to do it, when the clock outside began to strike the hour. I hesitated, wrapped the bird tighter. I could barely hear its muffled squawks, its rustling wings. If it was quiet it wasn't a threat, surely?

I weighted down the struggling canvas parcel with a couple of paintings and an old chair, and quickly ran the knife around the window frame. It swung open and a warm night breeze tickled my cheek. Here was freedom, mine to take. I looked down. The garden seemed far away. Could I do this? The wall of the house was flat and smooth but to my right was a drainpipe, I would have to reach it, climb down as far as the top of the garden wall... Then, as long as none of the party guests saw me, I might be able to inch along to the mews. I swallowed. I had no idea how I would get down from the wall into the mews without breaking one or both of my legs, but I decided I would find out when I got there. Wasn't the main thing to get out before anyone realized I had gone? Broken bones would heal.

I sat backwards on the windowsill, but the drainpipe was still far out of my reach. I would have to stand on the windowsill and reach across to grab it. I swallowed. Then I had another idea. I took off my jacket and tore off my shirt. I could use it as a kind of rope, looping it around the pipe to steady myself. But I still had to reach it. I took off my boots and hung them around my neck: bare feet on brick would be better.

I took a breath, stepped out on to the sill. For a moment I wished I could become one of those birds, just leap off and fly away. Back home, in Jamaica, the folk who came off the boats always wanted to fly back to their country, to some part of Africa: Bonny or Coromantee or Benin. I, being born on Jamaica, wanted only to fly back there. To Mount Vernon and Mamma, and then to the Maroon Country up in the mountains.

But if I fell now, there would be no going anywhere.

I reached across, stretched my hand as far as I could go and felt the pipe. I had no grip, I needed some foothold. A loose stone skittered off the windowsill and fell all the way down into the garden. My insides turned over. I retreated to the windowsill. Henry would have been across that gap in an instant, down the pipe and along the wall by now, shouting up at me that I was a landlubber.

I sat on the windowsill again. Perhaps if I was sitting, I could reach out and get my shirt, now twisted into a rope behind the pipe. I leaned out. Still not close enough. I needed to stretch a little more, just a little. . .

I fell.

For the shortest second I was holding nothing and it felt as if my heart had stopped. Then both my hands and all my nine fingers reached for that pipe and clung on for dear life.

My heart was pounding now, so loud I could hear nothing else. I gripped tightly and passed my shirt behind the pipe. Braced my two feet either side. I almost laughed with relief as I began to edge down. It was as easy to walk down the side of the building this way as it was to take a walk round the garden square! Henry would have been proud. I passed the third-floor window and the second. In the garden below, some of the guests were in the summer house: pale dresses and coats, shining hair, smiles and laughter. The windows were thrown open and in the glass panes I could see the flickering reflection of candlelight. There in a cream dress was the old mistress, deep in conversation with a white-wigged gentleman.

I was glad then I hadn't stuck Mr Bird with my knife. He was only a parrot, not a part of her at all.

At last, I reached the wall that divided the Barratts' house from their neighbours. I held my breath until I reached the back wall – and then I almost cried out, for there down below in the mews was a wagon!

My heart leaped like a flying fish and I thanked Mary and God and Mamma and Henry who must all be looking after me!

Then I smelled it. The wagon was the night-soil cart, full to the brim with the most unpleasant of human leavings. But at that moment I did not care. It would make my landing soft, and though my jacket might be past cleaning, I would not. I would be free and I would be alive. I swung both legs on to the mews side of the wall.

Sitting beside Mr Colley, Mr Furman looked up and caught my eye. The bottom half of his face was wrapped in a neckerchief, probably to keep out the smell. I grinned. I smelled only freedom.

Then I heard it. A screeching and a squawking and a flapping of wings. "Blood! Bones and blood!"

Mr Bird had freed himself.

I felt the air from his wings as he launched himself from the window. I looked down into the garden and spotted the old mistress. I could see the glint in her eye even from here. I jumped.

I thought I would retch, my eyes stung and my

hands scrabbled for the edge of the wagon, for some kind of grip before the night soil went over my face and down into my throat. I spluttered.

"Go!" I yelled, and the wagon jolted into life.

Then the door to the garden opened and the old mistress came hurrying across the cobbles, Mr Bird now on her shoulder screeching the alarm. Behind her was the young master, all pale blue satin coat and embroidered waistcoat.

"Footman!" he called and I was terrified again. "Get the boy!"

"Faster!" I yelled.

Then I had an idea. The cart was four sided, with a flap at the back that could be pinned up – to keep the soil in – or let down. The young master strode towards the cart, the old mistress picked up her skirts and scampered forward. I swear I had never seen her move so fast in all my life. As they came close their faces screwed up, no doubt with the smell. I seemed almost to have forgotten. At that moment, it could have been hibiscus, or orange blossom.

I pulled out the pins, first one side of the cart, then the other. Another jolt as the driver flicked the horses into a trot and the young master broke into a run, I gripped the front of the cart and watched as the night soil slid out of the back, spraying all over the young master's fine suit. Then I laughed out loud as the old mistress shrieked, her shoes slipping in the filth. She waved her arms like a windmill to steady herself, before going over on her bottom, head back in the road, wig falling off. The young master turned back to help her. He put out a stinking, wet hand to pull her up – and fell over too.

As the wagon turned out of the mews at full speed my last sight of them was of mother and son sitting in the road, covered from head to foot in human filth. I had never felt so happy in my whole life.

CHAPTER

The smell did not leave me for the next month, but I did not care. I was free, and away from the city. Not like those poor souls on the *Zong*, or the other slaves I had grown up with at Barratt Hall.

My first night of freedom is still so clear to me. Mr Colley drove us as fast as his poor horse would go, all across town in the dark, straight to The Cat and Mutton in the docks. Henry was watching for us outside the inn.

"Nat! As I live and breathe!" Henry ran forward

to hug me but stopped in his tracks as he saw I was covered in human filth. He laughed. "You do smell to heaven of all that's rank and rotten! But I am so glad to see you I will shake your hand anyway."

Henry took us round the back of the pub to a room where I washed and changed into some of his clothes.

"You are lucky to have found me," Henry said, as he led me into the main room. "I am sailing at the end of the week."

My heart sank a little then. But that night I ate and drank heartily. Mr Furman too, and we watched him dance and play the violin – Mary Lee was right, he could make the ship on his hat roll and sway exactly like a real three-master.

I had so much pork pie and good beer that my stomach stretched so full I could barely move. My head rang with the dancing tunes, and even though I still smelled of the night-soil cart I fell asleep by the side of the fire.

In the morning, the noise of the breeze making the ropes and sails on the river snap woke me early. I found myself in a bed under a roof made of thatch.

For a tiny moment I forgot myself. I was terrified

and did not know where I was. Then I remembered. I was free.

I stayed in The Cat and Mutton for a few days, just in case – although Henry agreed it would be better for me to get out of the city, one way or another. Then, on the third day of my freedom, Mr Furman returned with a new coat and breeches, a gift from the Sons of Africa. I was very grateful. The coat was wool and well made, the best I'd ever had, and a fine shade of blue like the sky back home before a storm. I put it on straight away.

"Now, Nathaniel," Mr Furman said sitting down at one of the inn's large wooden tables, "I have a proposal for you." He took out a letter. "This is from Mary."

He began to read. Up until then I had been thinking about going to sea with Henry, perhaps working a ship as a free man. I knew I was happier on land, but beggars could not always be choosers. Now though, as Mr Furman spelled out another, different future, I was so happy I almost wept.

"She has found me work with her brothers?" I said, just in case I had got it wrong.

"If you want it." Mr Furman nodded. "In the gardens they work at, out of town up in a village called Hackney, in. . ." He screwed up his face to read the words. "Mr Loddiges Nursery," he read aloud. "Mr Loddiges has many glasshouses and needs a lad with experience of exotic plants. . ."

I smiled so wide, Mr Furman laughed. "Boy, you look like the cat who got the cream never mind the mutton!"

And that was that. I took my leave of Henry, my first friend.

"I will learn my letters," I said. "I will, to write you."

"Then I'd better learn mine too!" he said. "We shall make it a race, the first to receive a letter buys the other a pork pie and a jug of beer this time next year!"

We shook hands. And I set off with Mr Furman for my new life. As we walked the road north into the countryside, I thought happily that I was no longer bought or sold or owned by anyone. Soon my labour would bring me money I could call my own. Mamma and Old Thomas would be so proud of me.

*

I saw Mary again on the Whitsun holiday when she came out for a picnic with her brothers. It was a glorious day. We set out across the fields together, me, Mary, Joshua, who worked in the glasshouse with me, and Benjamin her older brother, who worked with Mr Loddiges, talking to customers.

Joshua and I carried the basket between us. Up in the sky, swallows – for I knew what those birds were called now – sliced through the air.

"Your namesakes, the Barratts, will be back to Jamaica in a fortnight," she said.

I protested. "Oh, they are not my namesakes! Not any more. I will not be called by those that owned me!"

"Too right!" Joshua said, and Mary nodded.

"I'm Nat Thomas now. That's my name."

We found a patch of meadow and set out our feast. Mary had brought some beer and we had bought a good cheese from a dairy close to the gardens.

"How's Mr Bird?" I asked. I hoped perhaps he had flown away too.

"Oh, he's just the same, he went for Maggie when she was doing the fire up in the library, she's lucky to have all her fingers. She forgot herself and ran straight down the proper stairs instead of the servants' ones, bashed clean into Mistress Barratt, almost knocked her over!"

We all laughed, and Mary smiled. "How's work going?" she asked.

Joshua grinned. "Nat's teaching me all he knows, about the pineapples. . ."

"And Joshua's teaching me my letters," I replied.

Joshua nodded. "Nat's a fast learner!"

Mary smiled. "You'll be writing to Henry before he does I bet!"

I looked round. I was so lucky. Here we were in a meadow, the sun on our backs, the birds calling in the sky. My new life was still full of hard work, but I liked it. Sometimes, in the very early mornings, I would get up an hour before the others and help the night-soil men. Loddiges' garden used a lot of night soil to help the plants grow and Mr Colley was one of the men that delivered to us. Most of the other lads hated the job, Joshua specially said the smell made him vomit. I did not mind one bit. Mr Colley always brought news of Mr Furman and every time the cart opened and the dirt fell out on to our manure heap I saw, in my mind's eye, the Barratts covered in the stuff. I remembered again just how lucky I'd been to get away.

I raised my mug. "A toast to Mary!" She blushed and threw a handful of grass at me. "Thanks for your excellent help in my escape. And to friends and family far away."

I thought of Mamma and all the folk across the ocean, and Henry crossing the North Sea. And I blinked then; it felt as if I had the most enormous stone in my throat. Mary put a hand on mine.

"You will see your mother again," she said quietly. I nodded. It would just take time.

"I've got a toast!" Benjamin sat up. "To new friends!"

I raised my mug again. Mamma would be so pleased to see me here, among real friends. Working hard, free at last.

"Are you all right?" Mary asked.

I wiped my face. "It's only some of that grass you threw at me, got in my eye..."

Joshua drained his cup. "Enough toasts!" He got up. "Who can climb to the top of that beech tree the fastest?" He ran across the meadow and reached the bottom of the tree before any of us had even had a chance.

"Not fair!" Benjamin called.

I sped up and jumped for the low branch, but Benjamin still beat me to the top. I pulled myself up and sat down beside him, panting. I looked out across the city of London to the south. And I felt at home.

HISTORICAL NOTE:

THE SLAVE TRADE

Many countries and societies in history enslaved others in the past: the Romans, the Vikings, the Ottomans, the Chinese and the Incan empires to name a few. But until the British began enslaving African people in the seventeenth century, slaves were usually people captured in battle or conquest.

African enslavement was different. It was we British who modernized and industrialized the buying and selling of people to work in the hot climates of our new colonies in the Caribbean and

North America. It meant that huge fortunes were made by a few individual plantation owners, as workers did not have to be paid; slave owners could work men, women and children to death and just import new ones when they were needed. Enslaved people worked growing sugar cane, tobacco and, in North America, cotton. Walking round the streets of any big town in Britain today you can see the profits that came from the enslavement of millions of people over two hundred years. Art galleries – the Tate Modern and Tate Britain in London for example – and many fine country houses across the country were built using money that came from slave labour.

The slave system was made out to be a good thing to the ordinary British people. After all, argued the slave owners and traders, black Africans were not as intelligent, were not even as human, as white Europeans. This was, of course, all lies. But it kept the trade going and the money rolling in. It wasn't just the slave owners who profited, many industries flourished through the free labour including shipbuilding and gun manufacturing.

The public mood began to change after a series of important trials brought the treatment of slaves to the world's attention. One of these trials was that of the *Zong* – one of the most important turning points in the battle to end slavery. It meant that conditions on slave ships were printed in newspapers, talked about in churches and chapels, in coffee houses and pubs all across the country. Artists painted pictures about it, books and articles were written about it. Ordinary people began to see slavery for the inhumane trade it was. Some of the arguments and discussions in this story are based on real quotes from the *Zong* trial, and some have been simplified or imagined.

Eventually the actions of organizations like the Sons of Africa, and white abolitionists like Granville Sharp, John Clarkson, and later William Wilberforce, meant the government had to act.

The British trade in slaves was abolished in 1807, but the slaves in the colonies, like Jamaica, were not freed until 1833. There was a massive outcry among the slave owners. Not just plantation owners, but many middle-class Britons who invested in enslaved people as absentee owners: they used their money to invest in and buy enslaved people that they never saw or met, but whose labour directly profited them.

There was a massive backlash. No one wanted to lose money, so the British Government paid out compensation. The more slaves you owned the more money you received. The son of our former prime minister David Cameron's great-great uncle received what would amount to £3 million in today's money, for the two hundred and two slaves he owned.

The enslaved people received nothing. Not one penny. But at least they were free.

Slavery was not abolished in America until 1865, and not until 1888 in Brazil. During the three hundred years of the international slave trade, so many enslaved people were thrown overboard, dead and alive on what was called the Middle Passage that to this day, sharks follow the route of those ships, looking for more people to eat.

THE PEOPLE

NATHANIEL BARRATT and his owners are not real, but
their stories are inspired by real historical events.
Like Nathaniel, many enslaved people did
believe that slavery didn't exist in Britain. They
were sadly wrong – the notices advertising slaves
for sale that Mary reads out in the story are based
on real adverts.

OLAUDAH EQUIANO was a real person and had an
incredible life. He was captured and enslaved,
then went on to buy his own freedom. He
did write a book, and it was published as The
Interesting Narrative of the Life of Olaudah
Equiano. It became a best-seller and he
continued, alongside the Sons of Africa, to fight
for the abolition of slavery.

GRANVILLE SHARP was one of the first white English
men who campaigned to end the slave trade. His
writings were vital in changing people's minds,
and he worked tirelessly to change the law. He
died in 1813, after the British trade in enslaved

people had been abolished, but not before Great Britain ended slavery in our colonies.

SHADRACK FURMAN was a real man too, although the one in this story is really based on two men smooshed together. Shadrack Furman was one of the first black pensioners, which meant he was paid a pension for his service in the British army. He was an enslaved American who joined the British Army during the American War of Independence. The British promised freedom to every slave who fought for them, but when the British lost the war the ex-slave soldiers were shipped to Canada or Britain. There were so many black soldiers in London at the end of the eighteenth century that they were known as the St Giles' Blackbirds.

JOSEPH JOHNSON was the man who danced with a ship on his hat. He lived in London at the end of the eighteenth and beginning of the nineteenth century. He had a large model ship on his head and made his living dancing on the streets. A character based on him featured recently in a historical drama – only in the background though.

FRANCES SANCHO was real too. Her mother and father ran a grocer's shop in Mayfair. Her father, Ignatius, had been enslaved, worked in London and ran away. One of his owners left him money in their Will and he used it to buy his freedom. As a property owner he was entitled to vote in British elections, and in 1774 became the first black Briton to vote. He had six children, and the eldest was Frances.

THE MAROONS were people who escaped enslavement in Jamaica and set up villages and towns high up in the mountains. The hills were so high and the trees so dense that the British couldn't find them. There were several wars when the British tried to round up and capture the Maroons, but they never succeeded. One of their leaders was a famous woman fighter called Nanny. Today the only remaining Maroon settlements in Jamaica are semi-independent. The descendants of the original

Maroons speak a dialect that originates from the west coast of Africa, in what today is Ghana.

MR LODDIGES was a famous gardener who had one of the biggest collections of exotic plants in Britain. Before Kew Gardens built their huge glasshouses, his were the largest in the whole world. In Hackney nowadays there is no trace of his gardens, but he has a road and a massive estate of flats named after him.

TIMELINE

1562 John Hawkins is the first Englishman to voyage to Africa to participate in the transatlantic slave trade. He sells a total of 1,200 people to the Spanish in exchange for sugar, pearls and ginger.

1728 The first Maroon War in Jamaica. Groups of enslaved Africans rebel and defeat British forces in the fight for their freedom.

1760 A slave called Tacky leads a protest against the treatment of slaves on sugar plantations. Hundreds of slaves attack the plantations setting crops and sugar alight. In the end, Tacky is captured and killed.

1781 132 enslaved Africans are thrown overboard from the slave ship, *Zong*.

1783 The slave owners of the *Zong* attempt to claim money from their insurers, but the case is taken to trial and they lose.

1787 Ottobah Cuguano writes and publishes, "Thoughts and Sentiments on the Evil and Wicked Traffic of the Slavery and Commerce of the Human

Species". The Society for Effecting the Abolition of the Slave trade is founded.

1789 The Interesting Narrative of Olaudah Equiano is published.

1790 Parliament rejects William Wilberforce's first abolition bill.

1795 The Second Maroon War in Jamaica.

1807 Parliament passes the Abolition of the Slave Trade Act. People could no longer capture, buy or sell slaves. But slavery itself is still legal.

1833 Parliament passes the Slavery Abolition Act. This act gives all slaves in the Caribbean their freedom, but some other British territories have to wait longer. Ex-slaves in the Caribbean are forced to work for former masters for a low wage for a period of time, therefore slavery is not fully abolished in practice until 1838.

GLOSSARY

ABOLITIONIST A person in favour of formally putting an end to a practice or system

BROCADE A rich fabric woven with a raised pattern, typically with gold or silver thread

JUNKANOO A street parade with music, dance and costumes celebrated in many towns across Jamaica and the Bahamas

NABOB A wealthy person

ON THE LAM Someone who is on the run

PICKNEY A baby or child

PLANTATION A large farm on which crops such as coffee, sugar and tobacco are grown

SEDAN CHAIR A portable covered chair, usually carried by two men. Chairs were a popular mode of transport in the eighteenth century, as they could travel down lanes too narrow for carriages.

THE MIDDLE PASSAGE The journey where Africans, packed onto ships, were transported across the Atlantic to the West Indies. The voyage took between three to four months and the enslaved people lay chained in rows on the floor of the hold or on shelves that ran around the inside of the ships' hulls.

VERANDA A large open porch around the front and sides of a house

JIM ELDRIDGE

1918

COMING HOME

A GRIPPING FIRST-HAND ACCOUNT OF ONE OF THE MOST DANGEROUS TIMES IN HISTORY